# SUGAR FOR SUGAR

Seb Kirby is the author of the James Blake Thriller series (TAKE NO MORE, REGRET NO MORE and FORGIVE NO MORE), the psychological thriller EACH DAY I WAKE and the Raymond Bridges sci-fi thriller series (DOUBLE BIND). An avid reader from an early age - his grandfather ran a mobile lending library in Birmingham - he was hooked from the first moment he discovered the treasure trove of books left to his parents. He was a university academic for many years, latterly at University of Liverpool. Now, as a full-time writer, his goal is to add to the magic of the wonderful words and stories he discovered back then. He lives in the Wirral, UK.

By the same author

James Blake Series
TAKE NO MORE
REGRET NO MORE
FORGIVE NO MORE

Raymond Bridges Series
DOUBLE BIND

South Bank Series
EACH DAY I WAKE

Dear **Sarah**

Thanks for reading and reviewing SUGAR FOR SUGAR. Your interest is very much appreciated.

As you know, this is the prepublication version of the book and it's not yet fully corrected. Despite the best efforts of our editors, some errors have crept through:

Prologue - He takes his eyes **of** the road - off
p 10 "Just **sayin'"** – sayin'."
p 34 Fix **you** mind upon - your mind
p 42 We need to stay together **from** Kelly's sake - for
p 52 OK let's check them out." – "OK let's check them out."
p 156 I'll need police protection **from** me and my family - for
p 169 fallen from his hand and is **laying** there - lying.
p 182 he'd go so far as **so** rape her - to rape
p 183 that I'd tipped **of** Vince - off
p 190 "So we have to wait?" – extra line space.
p 204 The canal winds **it's** way – its

I hope this will not spoil your reading enjoyment. If you find any further errors, I'd be really grateful if you would email the details to me at seb.kirby@gmail.com or send a message via Facebook.

If you enjoy the book, please post a review at https://www.amazon.co.uk/Sugar-UK-Seb-Kirby/dp/1539120155 for the paperback edition and at http://www.amazon.co.uk/dp/B01M65SUXP after November 4th when the Kindle edition is made available.

With best wishes and thanks for your interest and help.

To Sarah

**Seb Kirby**

**SUGAR FOR SUGAR**

With best wishes

Sebo

For Alan and Jane Brooks

Trust is like that. You can break it for a good reason. But it still remains broken. (Harlan Coben)

# PROLOGUE

Mark Dankworth shifts the luxury SUV through the gears. He's late for the early morning meeting in London that he's tried his best to postpone. But no one will cut him any slack. So, here he is, peering through the pre-dawn November darkness at the twists and turns on the country road ahead and wishing he was already there.

In truth, he knows that the conditions outside are less than ideal. He should reduce his speed, given the poor visibility ahead, as pockets of fog lurk here and there in the hollows along the way. But why spend all that money on a top of the range performance vehicle if it isn't fit to cope with conditions like this? He'd be the one to pay if he failed to make the meeting on time.

He presses down harder on the accelerator and feels the reassuring surge of speed as the vehicle responds.

The song being played on the sound system is one he doesn't like. In fact, it annoys him. Why would his favourite band include something like that on what is otherwise a near perfect album? Better to skip that track, move on to the next.

He takes his eyes of the road for the briefest moment.

The sound system responds to a prod of his finger as the despised track is skipped.

His eyes return to the road.

He doesn't see it before it hits.

He feels it first. A dull thud as something collides with the front of the SUV, sending a shudder through the vehicle.

Then the blurred image of something heavy hurtling across the windscreen and disappearing behind him.

He grips the steering wheel, maintains onward direction. He is safe.

What was it? A dog? A badger?

Something tells him it was no dog, no badger.

Instinct tells him to apply the brakes. The vehicle slows and then stops.

The road around him is dark and still. There is no other traffic. No one about.

He unlocks the door, climbs out and begins to walk back along the road, towards whatever it is he's collided with.

There's something there, lying broken at the side of the road.

As he moves closer, he can tell that his instinct was right. It's no dog, no badger. He peers through the fog and sees that it's a young girl. A schoolgirl. Aged about ten. Somehow, her school bag is still with her, tangled now around her neck.

He panics. If he comes any closer, if he stays, they'll know it was him. When they analyse the scene, they'll discover that he was driving too fast. His life will be a mess.

He walks away. Back to the SUV. He knows he should phone to report the accident. They may still be able to save the girl. But then they will know it's him when they trace the call.

Someone else will find her. Make sure she gets the attention she needs. It will come out all right.

He feels secure again as the SUV envelops him in its comfort and responds to his need to escape.

Further down the road, there's the school bus the girl must have been heading towards.

As he passes, he hopes that no one will notice him.

# DAY 1

Five years later

# CHAPTER 1

I'm lost in a dark, dark place and, try as hard as I can, nothing helps me to understand.

When I seek answers, I see only broken shards of my past, flashes lighting this darkest of places for an instant, shining bright then fading as soon as they appear. Fragments of time, light and dark, great joy and great sadness, overlapping incidents in my life that I thought were lost forever.

And when I look again, it's as if what I've just seen has never existed.

I open my eyes and look around.

I'm sitting on a chair facing a woman who looks at me with care and concern. I say the only thing I need to say. "Where am I?"

She smiles at me. "You're at the Pinetree Medical Practice. I'm your doctor, Jane Wilson."

"How did I get here?"

"Your friend Marianne brought you here."

"Why would she do that?"

The doctor looks up from the notes she's making on her screen. "Because you're distressed." She pauses. "Can you tell me why you're feeling so anxious?"

I don't know why she's asking me this. Why should I trust anything she says when she won't tell me where I am?

"I don't know."

She keeps prying. "What can you tell me about the last twenty-four hours?"

"I can't. It's a blank."

"And that's why you're distressed?"

How could she know how this feels? I'm alone, lost in a cold emptiness with no way back home. Why can't she be straight with me?

"I don't know. Just tell me where I am?"

"You're with me, your doctor, Jane Wilson, at the Pinetree Medical Centre."

"How did I get here?"

"Your friend brought you. Do you remember her name?"

I'm so alone, how could she tell me I have a single friend in this world?

"I can't recall anyone bringing me here."

The doctor returns her attention to the screen. "I'm going to ask you some questions. They're going to help me find out what's wrong with you. Is that all right?"

"If it will help."

"OK. Tell me about yourself. What's your name?"

I know who I am. No one can take that away from me.

"Isobel Cunningham. Issy to my friends.'

"So, you won't mind if I call you Issy?'

"That's fine."

"And where do you live?"

I know that, too.

"Bentham Gardens. Apartment 21."

"And how old are you?"

"Forty-one next birthday."

God, I'm that old?

"Any brothers or sisters."

"I'm an only child."

"You're married?"

"To John. We're divorced."

"Any children?"

I feel a jolt of pain as she asks me this. I don't know why I should feel this way. I give her the only answer I can, the one I need to give.

"No children."

"And your parents?"

"Jenny and Tom. They're separated. She lives in Reading."

I can say this, but if I closed my eyes, I wouldn't see them. I'm not sure I've ever seen them.

"Spell WORLD."

Now she's saying I'm stupid. Who would ever want to ask a forty-one year old woman that?

"Why wouldn't I be able to spell it?"

"Just try."

"OK. W-O-R-L-D."

"That's fine. Tell me, Issy, do you suffer from migraine?"

"I don't know. I just want you to tell me where I am, how I got here."

The way she's acting, you'd think I'd just asked her that. Why can't she just level with me?

The doctor returns to her on-screen notes. "Your records show that in fact you do suffer from migraine. You've been managing attacks for the last three years, linked to periods of stress, as often as not."

"If you say."

"Where do you work?"

I can feel a pain tightening in my abdomen. A shadow of something or someone heading towards me.

"Ardensis Partners."

"And what's that?"

"It's an ad agency. I'm a consultant there."

"So there's the stress." The doctor takes in a deep breath. "Issy, you're confused and disorientated. You know all the details about who you are and about your family and where you live and work, yet you've lost your bearings somehow and that's what's making you feel so distressed." She points towards the examination couch. "There may be a physical cause. I'd like to take a look at you, if that's OK?"

Now she wants to touch me. There was someone who touched me last. Someone I trusted. Someone I don't want to trust again.

I remove my clothes and lie on the table. "I just want you to tell me why I'm here. Where I am."

She begins the examination by looking into my eyes and pressing at my head and neck, searching for a pain response. I feel none. "You haven't had a fall or been involved in any sports or physical activity that may have led to concussion?"

She doesn't understand.

"I told you. I don't recall. There is no past."

"Well, I can tell you that I don't see any signs of damage. And you don't respond as if that's the case. So, let's rule that out."

She makes the necessary checks on my heart rate and blood pressure.

"I see they're both elevated but maybe that's no more than to be expected."

She moves lower and checks my abdomen. She draws back in surprise at what she sees. "When did you last have sex?"

Why is she insisting on making this so personal? I just need her to tell me. Tell me what makes me feel like this?

"I told you, I can't recall. I can't recall anything going back. So I don't know if I've had sex, but I'm not in a relationship and I'm not the kind of person to have sex outside a relationship. You're casting doubt on me?"

"I'm only trying to get at the facts. You've had sex recently. Intense sexual activity. There's damage to your vagina and there's still some bleeding. Something violent. You still have pain there?"

I feel the shock of it as she touches me there.

"Yes."

"But you don't recall how or when it happened? Or who you were with?"

I was with him. The one who did this to me. The one I trusted. The one whose face I can't now recall.

"I'm trying to tell you. I don't know. Why don't you believe me?"

She asks me to put my clothes back on. "I want you to go with Nurse Armstrong to have some tests. She'll take a blood sample, some swabs and a urine sample. It won't take long."

The thought won't go away. The only thought. I need to know what he did to me.

# CHAPTER 2

While the nurse runs the tests, Dr Jane Wilson takes the opportunity to speak to Marianne French. "Tell me about Issy's state of mind and why you brought her here to the Medical Centre?"

"She was just sitting in the office, saying the same things, over and over. Where am I? Why am I here? I've never seen anyone as confused as that. I thought she must be having a breakdown. Isn't that what it is?"

"I don't think so. But there's one question I need you to answer. The day before, how was she?"

"She was fine. Concerned about some problem she wouldn't tell anyone about, but she was her normal self. That's what's so shocking about the way she is now. The sudden change."

Jane Wilson ticks the last box on the diagnostic dialogue on her screen. *Independent verification of the change in the state of mind of the patient.* She turns to Marianne. "Will there be anyone to take care of Issy when she leaves here?"

"We're close colleagues. I'll do all I can but there are things back at the office that won't wait."

"She has no one else who's close?"

"Issy lives alone."

"OK. There's King's College Hospital at Camberwell. I'll refer her there for a short stay." Dr Wilson pauses. "She needs time and rest somewhere safe. They can provide that."

Marianne nods. "You said short stay?"

"What your friend has is uncommon but not as rare as many suppose. She has posttraumatic stress, that's for sure. But, as a result of the rape, I think it might be more than that."

Marianne stiffens. "Issy was raped?"

"Didn't you know? She's suffered a violent sexual attack. And she's showing many of the signs associated with that. But, as I said, I don't think that's enough to explain the almost complete disorientation she's showing. I specialized in neuroscience and I know more than many GPs, so Issy is lucky in that respect. I've come across half a dozen cases like it in my time."

"So, not just the effects of the attack?"

Dr Wilson shakes her head. "I've ruled that out. I'm more or less certain there's a serious problem with her memory. They'll find out more at the hospital."

As Marianne prepares to leave, Dr Wilson asks her to remain seated. "There's something I need to ask. Is there anything else that might have a bearing on her condition? Do you know of any recent changes in Issy's life, either at home or at work?"

Marianne looks down. "I didn't want to be the one to mention this. There's been a death where we work. At the Agency. The police are investigating."

"And you think Issy may have been affected by that?"

"We're all affected by it."

"And she knows?"

"It hasn't registered. Nothing's getting through to her."

Marianne stands to leave. "I've changed my mind. I'll go with her to the hospital. Whatever's happening back at Ardensis will just have to wait."

# CHAPTER 3

Everyone is kind and caring. But I have no idea why I'm here, wrapped in this grey blanket, lying on this stretcher while the ambulance picks its way through the London traffic.

I try to tell myself it must be because of the pain in my abdomen, that this is what makes me a case for treatment, but I know, deep down, it's more than that. It's about all that I can't remember.

Now I'm aboard a trolley being wheeled past a sign that says *King's College Hospital.* A male porter checks over the paperwork clipped to the back of the trolley and shouts out what he sees to his colleague pulling me along from the front.

"Isobel Cunningham. Psychological Trauma. For Room 21. Short Stay."

So, I'm here for trauma. At least they have that right.

They take me to a well-furnished room with a bed and couple of chairs for visitors.

A female nurse, who tells me her name is Elizabeth Hewitt, is waiting. "Mr Mortimer is on his ward rounds in the main hospital and won't be able to see you for at least an hour. The notes say you should rest. Why don't you lie down, maybe get some sleep if you feel like it."

It's broad daylight. Why would I want to sleep?

"By tomorrow you'll be feeling a whole lot better."

I don't have a yesterday, why would I have a tomorrow?

When the nurse leaves, I lie back on the bed, on top of the covers.

I stare at the ceiling.

Why have they brought me here? What's wrong with my own place?

A buzzing noise comes from the bag at the foot of the bed.

That must be my bag. My phone.

I retrieve the phone and look at the screen. A Twitter alert.

So this is me. This is what I am right now. What I have become.

I lie back on the bed and begin scrolling through the messages.

The screen tells me I have three hundred and thirty-three friends. There are faces and names.

How did I ever get to know so many people?

I stare at my profile picture.

I look happy enough. Somewhere near a beach with the sun shining on my wavy blonde hair from a blue sky and reflecting highlights in my grey-green eyes. Why wouldn't I feel happy with my sunglasses sat on my head like that?

But I'm not feeling happy. Everything is wrong and it's my fault. This feeling of guilt is something I can't control. It's consuming me, taking over my whole being.

I know I have shake myself out of this.

I return to the messages on the phone and stop at the image of a bearded man with round frame glasses and the name Colin Tempest alongside.

Someone I should know. Should know well. From Ardensis. Working next to me. Why do I feel so let down by him? Someone who asked for my help. I know he was responsible in some way for how I'm feeling. So why can't I say to myself that I know what he's done?

I scroll further down and come to the picture of Mary Duggan.

There she is. What's her message saying?

'You can always depend on me.'

I read every message that comes from Mary. It doesn't make any kind of story I can understand. But I know she's my friend.

I lie back on the bed and start to cry. Somehow the procession of faces on the phone has made things worse. All these people I'm supposed to know but can't understand, can't recall ever having met.

Yet I feel drawn back to them.

It's a shadow of my self and I know it's all I have.

I don't know how long what I've just discovered will last. If it's connected with the emptiness I feel, I don't think I'll be able to retain it for long.

I find the notes app on the phone and begin to type.

*Why did Colin need my help?*

*Mary is a good friend.*

# CHAPTER 4

Ardensis Partners is situated in a smart part of Islington, close to Old Street Roundabout, where the high-tech start-ups are only outnumbered by the profusion of coffee bars and restaurants that service them. It is part of an ever-expanding hub that is transforming how hi-tech business is carried out in London. Some are calling the area Tech City and likening it to Silicon Valley.

But Ardensis isn't hi-tech, it's advertising and DI Stephen Ives doesn't like creatives. He makes no attempt to disguise the fact. "There's only one thing worse than an ad agency and that's a successful one that's full of clever people who make more in a month than we do in a year by dreaming up stuff that you or I wouldn't waste the time of day on."

DS June Lesley, driving the police car en route to Old Street and struggling to find a way through the dense London traffic, doesn't rise to the bait. "If you ask me, Steve, your prejudice is showing. The world moves on. These people come up with bright ideas, make money and they pay their taxes. What's wrong with that?"

"And they do that by preying on the gullibility of the average citizen."

"Who exists mainly in your own head. Who's average? No one. I thought you knew. Everyone's a fully rounded individual these days."

"If I thought less of you, June, I'd say you were putting me on?"

"Just sayin'"

Ives changes the subject as they draw closer to their destination. "So, what do we have?"

SEB KIRBY

"Michael Aspinal. Age thirty-six. Senior Executive at Ardensis Partners. Found dead in his office at 7.30 AM by building security on their morning rounds. The medic at the scene diagnosed a massive heart attack as the cause of death."

"Then why are we needed?"

"The local police who were called flagged up the death as *unexplained sudden*. And you know what the Commissioner's policy is?"

"All unexplained sudden deaths to be investigated. Does he really think his knighthood depends on meeting productivity targets one hundred per cent?" He paused. "No need to answer that, June. It's true and I don't want to know any more about it."

"So we investigate."

"Who was it? Who was at the scene?"

"Pilkington."

Ives lets out a stifled yell. "The man's an idiot. I don't expect he looked too deeply into what he found."

"Every little helps."

"Might as well go pee in the sea."

Lesley smiles. "I don't know how to keep track on how that mind of yours works. Where did that come from?"

"One of my mother's sayings. Every little helps, said the old woman as she peed in the sea. You must have heard it?"

"I don't think people bother much with sayings these days, sir."

"Don't call me sir."

"Yes, Steve."

"So, where is Aspinal now?"

"The body is on the way to Westminster Morgue for post mortem."

Ives shivers, recalling how much he loathes the very mention of the place. "I get it. Unexplained sudden death. Post mortem. One hundred per cent. Commissioner's knighthood." He pauses. "I'm not becoming cynical, am I, June?"

"You? Why would anyone think that?"

Ives looks Lesley full in the face. "There's a glint in your eye, June. Come on, level with me. You know something. Something that means you *want* to be here."

"Not really."

11

"Tell me."

"Call it a feeling, Steve. Just a feeling."

# CHAPTER 5

A doctor in a white coat comes in. His name is Mr Mortimer.

Why is he called mister when he's a doctor?

Nurse Hewitt stays while Mr Mortimer examines me.

Why is he asking me so many questions? Who I am. What do I recall?

The only thing he needs to know is that I have no past and no future.

And what I need to know is why I'm here.

When the questions end, he sits on the edge of the bed and tells me what he's found.

"Isobel, I can't disagree with the diagnosis of your GP.

"Call me Issy."

"Sorry, Issy. Jane Wilson studied here at King's College before she opted for general practice. She knows your condition well. Your memory will improve. You just need time. You're feeling more comfortable now, I'm sure."

"If you say so, doctor."

He's trying but he can't know how this feels.

"I want you to take resting seriously. Let the healing process take its course. I've told the hospital that you're to have no visitors until tomorrow at the earliest, to make sure that your recovery is not disturbed."

He holds my hand. "Don't worry. Things will start to look much better by the morning."

I stare back into his caring eyes and begin to sob. "I'm sorry. So sorry to be putting everyone to all this trouble when what's happening is all my fault."

He offers me a tissue from the box beside the bed. "That's no way feel about this, Issy. Hold on. You will feel better."

I wipe away the tears. "Just tell me why I'm here."

# CHAPTER 6

Marianne French paces the floor. She knows she can't stay at the hospital with Issy much longer. She's needed back at Ardensis.

When the doctor rushes past she just catches sight of his name badge in time.

"Mr Mortimer. I understand you're treating Isobel Cunningham."

He looks to be on the point of saying that he's on an urgent call when he stops and takes Marianne to one side.

"She's stable and on a path to recovery but it will take time."

"Dr Wilson tells me it's not a breakdown."

He shakes his head. "No, she's right about that. Your friend's symptoms point to a condition we call temporary global amnesia. TGA. Isobel is confused and disorientated, yet she knows who she is, where she lives, where she works, all the factual details about herself and her life. But looking back, she has no memory and, what's worse, she's finding it impossible to make new memories. That's the reason she keeps asking where she is and how she got here and why she's here. If she's told, the memory doesn't stick, it's no surprise that she's distressed and confused."

"You said more or less certain?"

"There's a lot about TGA we still don't understand. It's more common in women than men and in people over the age of forty. It's sometimes connected with people who have migraine, but that's not always the case. In others it's connected with immersion in very cold water or with a sudden and violent series of events. So, any diagnosis involves a degree of uncertainty."

"TGA, it's permanent?"

"Thank goodness, no. And that's how it differs from similar symptoms brought on by the damage to the head, say in an accident, or in the case of a nervous breakdown. The main effects of TGA clear within twenty-four to forty-eight hours. The patient will gradually rediscover the ability to recall past events, most often one by one, with the most important coming first. But she may or may not ever recall the most recent events, particularly if they're connected with trauma. And the ability to form new memories will return, too. There's no need for any specific medication. She just needs peace and quiet and plenty of rest. However, the effects of the sex attack may take much longer to come to terms with."

"That's a complication?"

"It is. I'm as concerned about the long-term effects of the sexual assault. She's been damaged physically but that will heal. She needs to take advice on the likelihood of long-term emotional damage and how this can lead to feelings of worthlessness, even guilt that she was somehow responsible for what happened. That might take a whole lot more getting over than her short-term memory problems. She mustn't be afraid to take the help that's offered."

The call responder in Mortimer's coat pocket begins beeping. "Look, I have to go. I can see you're a good friend to be here with her like this. As she mends, stay with her and remind her that she's going to need her friends around her."

"Can I see her?"

He frowns. "I don't think that's going to help at the moment. It's best for her recovery that she's left to work through this herself for the next twenty-four hours. I'm going to be transferring her to the Haven, our secure unit for victims of sexual abuse. The police liaise with us there. They'll make sure any forensic evidence hasn't been missed and we'll continue to look after her medical needs at the same time. They'll also have officers trained in counselling people who've been through what Issy has experienced. I'm sure they'll be able to help. Ask to visit her tomorrow."

# CHAPTER 7

I'm lying still in the bed with only the distant sounds of the hospital around me to fill the emptiness I feel within.

It's a new bed in a new place not far from the old one, in a place they told me is called The Haven, but that means little to me.

My eyes are closed, yet a glimpse of the splinters of my past keeps forming itself, faint at first, then with increasing definition and complexity. Ghosts that I don't want to let in.

The anatomy of my guilt, revealing itself whether I want it or not.

*I'm with my mother, Jenny. In our home in Reading. I'm fourteen. My mother has a worried look. Something terrible has happened in I'm the one who is the centre of attention.*

*My mother is crying. "What did you have to tell your father for?"*

*I'm struggling to understand. "I didn't do anything. I just said you went out last night looking nice."*

*She's shaking her head. "I asked you not to tell him. I asked you to say I was here with you all evening. Why couldn't you do that one simple thing for me?"*

*"I don't see why it matters that much. He asked me. My father asked me. Did you really expect me to lie?"*

*"You're old enough now, Issy, to know what would happen if you told him the truth."*

*"I don't know what you mean."*

*She's embracing me. "Now Tom's got the excuse he needs to leave us, to get a divorce. I tried to tell him that Jeff is only a friend but he wouldn't believe me."*

The ghosts depart and it's as if I've never seen them.

I don't know if I'll ever see them again.

Nurse Hewitt comes in to check my pulse and blood pressure. She notes the results on the chart at the foot of the bed.

"You'll soon be feeling better."

I try to smile but a smile will not come.

When she's gone I make a note on the phone.

*I should have trusted my mother.*

# CHAPTER 8

Marianne French arrives back at Ardensis Partners to find two police officers at her door.

The tall younger-looking one speaks first. "Didn't mean to disturb you. My name is Ives. Detective Inspector Ives." He gestures towards the much shorter woman beside him. "And this is Detective Sergeant Lesley. We're here concerning Mr Aspinal."

Marianne invites them in. "It's been a great shock to everyone here I'm sure you'll understand."

Ives frowns. "No doubt he'll be missed." He pauses, looking for a response.

Marianne tries to sound convincing. "Of course."

A look passes between Lesley and Ives that says: *Not much love lost there.*

Marianne is trying to gather her thoughts. "You'll have to excuse me, Inspector. Mike's heart attack isn't the only shock we've had today. I'm just back from hospital. Isobel Cunningham, one of our consultants, is being treated at the King's College for acute stress. Her doctor says Issy was attacked and raped."

Lesley looks concerned. "It's been reported?"

Marianne nods. "I think so. Issy is too traumatised to do that herself but her doctor, Jane Wilson, is very thorough. I'm sure she will."

Lesley continues. "Do you know where and when the rape took place?"

Marianne shakes her head. "That's the really troubling thing. She can't tell anyone what happened. Dr Wilson says it will take time before we'll know the answer to any of that."

"Tell us about Isobel Cunningham?"

"Well. There's not much to tell. She's been here for three years now. Reliable, dependable. Gets on well with everyone. And she's a good personal friend."

"And outside the office?"

"Lives alone. No partner. No children. I guess that's the way she wants it to be."

Ives tries not to show his irritation but can't help interrupting. "Once the attack on your colleague is reported it will be sent to our Sapphire team. That's our rape and serious sexual assault unit. They're specialists. They'll handle the enquiry sensitively, I can assure you of that." He pauses. "But to come to the point and get back to business, the reason why we're here. You're OK about talking to us about Mr Aspinal? We could talk again tomorrow if you need to."

Marianne shakes her head. "No. I'll be all right. What else do you need to know?"

Ives takes over the questioning while Lesley makes notes.

"Did Mr Aspinal often spend time in his office late at night?"

"What do you mean?"

"Well, he was found at 7.30 AM this morning but the reporting officer says he was still dressed like he'd not been home from the night before. And when the officer touched the body, it was cold. Like Mr Aspinal had died in the office during the night."

"I don't know anything about that, Inspector. It would have been unusual behaviour for Mike, or anyone else here for that matter, but not unprecedented."

Ives shoots a glance back at Lesley that says: *Expect nothing less from the creatives.*

He presses on. "OK. We'll need the security camera footage for the building. I'm sure that will shed light on Mr Aspinal's movements."

"Is that everything, Inspector?"

"No. We also need background on the company. You know, how the agency works, who the main players are, that sort of thing."

Marianne knows that her reputation as being the one you knows everything that happens in the office must have preceded her. But this is a terrain on which she feels more comfortable. "Where do you want me to start?"

"Tell us what you know about the business."

"There's not much to say. Ardensis Partners was set up by Vincent Blakemore, the current CEO. He saw the need for an ad agency that could be responsive to the needs of the new high-tech businesses forming in London, a company specializing in bringing them to a wider audience." She pauses and smiles. "I hope this doesn't sound too much like the company brochure?"

Ives responds. "So that's why you're here in Old Street?"

"It is. But what you see here didn't happen overnight. Vince went through hard times getting started. He had to put his own house on the line to keep the company afloat in the early days. He had to fight and fight hard to make it happen."

"So, without him there would be no Ardensis."

"That's certain. And it's taken its toll. Vince has been in need of a rest for a long time and for far too long he wouldn't listen. But we finally convinced him he should take a break. You know, to recharge and start all over when he comes back."

"So that's why he's not here?"

"That's right. He finally agreed to take a three-month break. Travel in the States. He has family over there. He's not expected to be back for another month."

"Who's been in charge while Mr Blakemore is away?"

"That's Mike. Mike Aspinal." Marianne looks away. "Excuse me, Inspector, it's still a struggle to talk about him like this after what's happened to him."

Ives softens his voice. "I understand. Just a few more questions. Where is Mr Blakemore now?"

"He's still in the States."

"You've told him about Aspinal's death?"

"We're trying to reach him."

Lesley pauses from taking notes. "So, how was Mr Aspinal when he was in charge?"

Marianne leans forward and lowers her voice. "I don't want to speak ill of the dead but if you don't get this from me you'll certainly get it from just about anyone else here. To put it simply, he's been a disaster. You know what they say. All power corrupts."

Ives cuts in. "It went to his head?"

"In Mike's case you might say that." She pauses. "Oh, don't get me wrong, Vince thought he'd made a good choice when he appointed Mike as acting CEO while he was away. But from the start it's been one of the worst decisions he's ever made."

Ives resumes the questioning. "How so?"

"Well, you know how some people get carried away when they think they've reached the top. Start to see the world and everything that happens in it as somehow a mark of their own importance. Well Mike had that in spades. He's been a rules hound."

"Rules hound?"

"You know, the rules are the rules and he's the man to implement them, like he'd lose a big chunk of his ego if the smallest regulation was broken and no one paid the price."

Ives gives a knowing smile. "We have a few like that of our own back at the station. Goes with the turf."

Marianne insists. "No it's more than that. More pathological. With Mike, the rules had to be enforced no matter what the consequences. Where a good manager would have cut people a little slack if they stepped out of line, he didn't see it that way. In the end you couldn't avoid thinking he enjoyed it. Enjoyed using his power over everyone."

"You have an example?"

"We had a young intern, Mark Walker, fresh out of university. A bright lad, good imagination, but as green as they come. Mike gave him twenty-four hours to come back with a profile of a potential client but he was an hour late with the report. Mike dismissed him. When he asked for a reference to try to get another post in advertising somewhere else, Mike refused and told him he'd never work in the industry again. And that's just one example. He started making us all account for our time, hour by hour. He started interfering in everything that everyone did, looking for what he called infringements in company policy and practice. He said he was determined to prove we could be more efficient than when Vince was in control."

"So, he didn't exactly make himself the most popular kid on the block."

"You can say that again. From being the kind of place where everyone was giving extra in exchange for setting their own agenda, the agency changed so that everyone was looking over their shoulder, making sure Mike wasn't about to move against them for some infraction of rules that most never knew even existed."

"And Mr Aspinal didn't mind being disliked?"

"He thrived on it. Took it as a sign of his power over us all. That he was doing his job properly."

"And don't you think the stress got to him? Brought on the heart attack?"

She nods. "I guess that must have played a part after all."

# CHAPTER 9

*It's our wedding day.*

*I want to tell anyone how much I love this man.*

*The moment I saw him, I knew he was the one.*

*He's looking sheepish, talking to one of his friends as he tries to pluck up the courage to come over and talk to me at the crowded party.*

*It isn't the most original chat up line. "How come you know Eleanor?"*

*Yes, Eleanor. The one holding the party. Her birthday. Friends invited.*

*"We were at school together."*

*He's nervous and trying not to show it. "In London?"*

*"Yes. Wandsworth Common."*

*"You'd need a lottery win to live there now."*

*I'm smiling. "It wasn't as posh back then."*

*And that was it. John. The love of my life.*

*Walking down the aisle to stand beside him.*

*Saying our vows.*

I open my eyes and these visions rush away and hide where I may not find them again. It takes a moment before I understand that I'm still here in this sterile bed in the hospital waiting, hoping for someone to bring this nightmare to an end.

I pick up the phone and make a note.

*John, how did I ever lose you?*

# CHAPTER 10

It has to be done. Yet that doesn't make it any easier for Stephen Ives. He dreads these visits to Horseferry Road. Each time he sets foot in Westminster Mortuary is no better than the last.

He recalls the last time he was here, to witness a post-mortem on young Cathy Newsome, too long in the ground while they searched for the killer. The sickness in his stomach, that no one suspects he's capable of given his twenty-five years in the force, is as strong as ever. He knows that no amount of familiarity with the business of this place will ever alter the grief he feels at the sheer carelessness of the loss of each life.

Lesley parks their vehicle close the entrance.

Time to go inside. Get this done.

"Who's the duty pathologist?"

Lesley doesn't blink. "Andrea Julienne."

The same pathologist that attended to Cathy. Someone up there is taking care of the irony of repetition, after all.

Inside they find Julienne working on the body of Michael Aspinal, laid out on the steel examination table before them.

Julienne looks up as she hears them come in. "I was sure it was a heart attack, pure and simple, until I found this."

She uses a green laser pointer to highlight the small area of bruising on Aspinal's back, between the shoulder blades. "Not just a bruise, if you look closely."

Ives comes forward and stares at the region Julienne is indicating. "I don't see much."

"Look even closer. A small puncture mark where a needle has entered."

"OK. I can see it now. The kind of thing you get if you have a blood test or an immunization jab."

"Exactly."

Ives can tell that Julienne has much more to say and that she must have been busy using the state-of-the-art analysis techniques of the mortuary to check further. "So what have you found?"

"An increased level of potassium in the blood. Way over normal, even after the effects of a heart attack."

Ives interrupts. "Hold on. You're saying you would expect to find potassium?"

"Yes. By the time the heart stops, you expect to find some increase in potassium levels in the blood. But the potassium in Aspinal's blood is off the scale."

"Potassium. Doesn't sound too lethal. Don't people with high blood pressure use it instead of salt?"

"They do, but quantities like this never get into the blood. They'd die like he did if that happened."

"So, you're saying he was injected with something, something containing potassium?"

"Yes, most likely potassium chloride. Dissolves in water just like salt. Odourless. Colourless. If I told you it was one of the main ingredients in the toxic mix they use in the States for execution by lethal injection, would that help?"

Ives is getting the picture. "Aspinal was killed that way?"

"I'm saying *yes*. Potassium, once it's in your blood, takes over from the sodium that's essential in your body for life, passing signals from one neuron to the next to keep you alive. Without sodium, your heart can't function. It doesn't know how to beat. You suffer a massive heart attack. That's what happened here."

"What are the chances this was self inflicted?"

Julienne shakes her head. "I'd say close to zero. Why would he go for the area between the shoulder blades when he could have chosen a readily accessible place like and arm or a leg? No, the man was killed."

"No signs of any other damage, like he was beaten or tied up before he died?"

"None at all. It's more as if he was stabbed in the back with the syringe and had no time to react while the potassium chloride was pumped into him."

"Can you be confident about the time of death?"

Julienne frowns. "That could have been more accurate if I'd been called to the crime scene, but since the attending medics assumed it was a straightforward case of heart attack, there was no reason for me to be there. By the time the coroner decided that this was an unexplained death that required a post mortem, precious time had been lost."

"So, what can you say?"

"Well, the body is back to ambient temperature so he's been dead at least twelve hours. But from the progress of the rigor mortis, I'd say something longer than that. Something more like between fifteen and nineteen hours."

Ives looks at his watch and begins counting back. "That means between 12.00 midnight and 4.00 AM on the 14th. Valentine's Day. You can't give us a narrower time window than that?"

Julienne shakes her head. "How much closer than that do you want? Even that's pushing the bounds of certainty."

Ives thanks her. "Good work. I'll need your report as soon as."

He can't wait to get back to the car.

He just needs to get away from this place where there is no such thing as good news.

He now knows they have a murder case on their hands.

Lesley walks alongside him as they leave the mortuary. "Not what you expected, sir?"

Ives agrees. "Without Julienne we may never have known it was murder." He pauses. "And, June, you must have been as affected by that as much as I was. I thought you agreed to not call me *sir?*"

# CHAPTER 11

A sound from somewhere far off, getting closer all the time.

I open my eyes. The phone is ringing.

I pick it up and look at the image on the screen.

The bearded man again, the one with the name Colin Tempest next to his photo. Someone I must know. I have to answer.

I take the call.

A male voice. "Issy, I've been trying to reach you but you haven't been answering."

I can't concentrate on what he's saying. I say the only thing that comes to me. "Who are you?"

"Don't be foolish, Issy. It's Colin. We need to talk."

It's a voice I've heard before.

"I can't talk now."

He's insistent. "I can come over. Where are you?"

I look around the room. It doesn't look familiar. I say the only thing I can. "I don't know. I don't think I've ever been in this place before."

There's a new note of concern in his voice. "I'll find a way to help you, to make amends if you just tell me where you are."

Make amends? So he's done something to me. He thinks the reason I'm not talking to him is because of that.

"Tell me what you did to me."

"I'm sorry, Issy. I'm really sorry but he left me no choice. You were the only one I could turn to, the only one who might have convinced him to change his mind."

"What happened to Mike?"

"You know what happened to him, Issy. He died. A heart attack. You must know that. Why are you trying to pretend that none of this has happened?"

Mike is dead. I must have known that.

Is this the reason for these feelings of guilt I can't control?

"I'm not pretending."

He pauses for longer than he should. "The police have been here. What if they start interviewing everyone? It won't be long before they get round to you and me. Whatever else is said, I need you to promise you won't reveal our secret. You know it would ruin me and my family."

I don't know any secret. Why would he think I did?

"If anyone asks it's not going to be a problem for me to tell them I don't know."

"Thank you, Issy. I knew I could depend on you."

I stare again at the profile picture of the bearded man.

He wants me to trust him again but I know I can't.

His voice breaks into my thoughts once more. "Look, Issy. I've got to go. Something urgent. Thanks for your help. Thanks for being so understanding. Thanks for everything."

He closes the line.

I know that what's been said won't last long in my mind. I make a note on the phone.

*Mike is dead.*

*Why do I feel so guilty?*

*Colin behaves like he owes me.*

# CHAPTER 12

Ives and Lesley return to Old Street and seek out Marianne French.

She's surprised. "I wasn't expecting to see you again so soon, Inspector."

Ives grimaces. "We have more questions."

"What's changed?"

"It's likely that Mr Aspinal didn't die of natural causes."

"Someone killed him?"

"That's what the post mortem is telling us."

The colour drains from Marianne's face as Ives begins to question her. "Did anyone threaten Mike Aspinal?"

"Not that I know of. He didn't allow much room for disagreement. As I told you, Inspector, Mike's regime was disciplinarian. Complain and you're out."

"So there are plenty who'd be pleased to see him go?"

"I wouldn't say that."

"We'll need details of everyone who works here."

Marianne nods. "That's no problem, I can print you a list."

He turns and looked towards the office door. "We're going to need to check out Mike Aspinal's emails, social media."

Marianne shows them into the CEO office and gestures towards Aspinal's computer. "You'll find his logins in the back of the diary."

Ives shoots a look at Lesley that says: *Why do they all do that?*

He presses on. "We'll need to take the computer away. I'll get someone to call with a warrant and pick it up." He pauses. "Tell me, has this room been used since Aspinal's body was taken away?"

Marianne shakes her head. "Once your police colleagues left, it was locked and it's remained that way."

"Nothing's been removed?"

"Not to my knowledge."

"OK, we need some time to look around."

Once Marianne leaves, Ives and Lesley put on surgical gloves and begin searching the office, taking care to check on the contents of the desk drawers.

When they finish and find nothing of interest, Ives turns to Lesley. "No sign of the syringe."

"As expected."

"We'll need to see Pilkington's report on what he found here. I don't expect it will reveal much, but we need to check."

As they're leaving the room, Ives turned to Lesley. "Marianne French didn't ask how Aspinal died. What do you make of that?"

"Maybe she was too shocked by what you told her."

"Or perhaps she knows more than she wants us to believe."

They return again to Marianne French who hands Ives the list of Ardensis personnel.

Ives thanks her. "We now need a space to interview them."

Marianne shows them to a large room further along the corridor from her office. "You're welcome to use the Board Room. We have no meetings planned."

They spend the afternoon interviewing the Ardensis personnel.

Ives promises himself that he won't let on about his disdain for the advertising creatives before him. But, as he expects, they are indeed a bunch of misfits and drop outs somehow earning a fat living from the gullibility of the public. None has much to add to the scenario of the killing. Just like Marianne French, they are shocked by what has happened to Mike Aspinal. They are even more puzzled as to why the police are now investigating. If any of them has anything to hide, they are making a good fist of it.

At the end of the afternoon, Ives confers with Lesley and tries to keep the *I could have told you that* tone out of his voice. "So, did we find anything new?"

Lesley looks down. "Nothing of note."

"They all hated Aspinal."

"On a scale of one to ten, I'd say a ten."

"But we already knew that."

"Just one missing. Colin Tempest. Marianne French says he's gone home ill."

"Get him to come in, as soon as."

"And, or course, there's also Isobel Cunningham."

"Of course."

"We should talk to her. For completeness, you understand, Steve."

"When there's time. When there's time."

# CHAPTER 13

*Snow is coming down, building great drifts against the garden walls each side of the street.*

*All I can see from the window are swirling white flakes driven in hard on a biting winter wind.*

*There's unbelievable pain. The contractions have started and they're coming stronger now and closer together.*

*I'm calling out for John. He's somewhere in the basement, building a crib for our first born in the workshop he has down there.*

*And here she is. In my womb, demanding to come into the world. Now. Right now.*

*I'm shouting. "John. The baby's coming!" But he can't hear me.*

*It's a steep flight of stairs to the basement. I'm watching myself struggling down, each step a jolt of pain as the contractions keep coming.*

*I'm taking deep breaths. My mind is centred on one thing.*

*Make it to John. He'll take me to the hospital.*

*I'm reaching the doorway to the basement workshop.*

*I'm calling out. "John. I need you!"*

*He appears and knows straight away. "OK. Deep breaths. I'll call an ambulance."*

*"No time. I need you to take me to the hospital. Now!"*

*"You sure?"*

*"The baby's coming."*

*It's cold outside. I pull the blanket round me. The snow is piling higher with each passing minute.*

*At first the old Ford won't start. It's sputtering and complaining as John struggles to get it going.*

*Then it fires and we're off into the cold, white whirlwind that's swirling all around us.*

*The maternity hospital is at the top of the steepest hill for miles around. Why put a hospital up there?*

*The storm has caught the authorities on the hop. There's been no time for salting the roads. The snowploughs haven't yet made it to our end of town. And the blizzard is building all the time.*

*John has the windscreen wipers on at full speed yet all we can see ahead is a swirling whiteness. So, we're going slow. Much too slow.*

*The contractions are stronger than ever. I'm preparing myself for the thought that our baby is going to be born in the back seat of the car. And that frightens me. I won't know what to do. I don't think John will know what to do. And there will be no one else around now that the blizzard has taken over everyone's lives.*

*I'm breathing harder and deeper now. Trying to concentrate on what they've taught me in the prenatal classes. Keep calm. Deep breaths. Fix you mind upon that beautiful, calm Caribbean island where the sun is always shining.*

*But the contractions keep coming. Stronger and faster with every breath I take.*

*My waters breaking. Feeling the warm, sticky fluid running down my legs.*

*John is trying to coax the old Ford to the top of the steep, steep hill that leads to the hospital. I can hear and feel the wheels slipping and sliding on the compacted ice and snow that's taken over the roadway. I fear we're not going to make it up the hill and the Ford will give out its last gasp before we reach the top.*

*Somehow, we've made it and we're passing through the hospital gates and onto the apron where the snow has been cleared.*

*Orderlies appear and lift me from the back seat of the car onto a trolley. They wheel me into the hospital.*

*A tough looking woman in green scrubs takes one look at me and asks for a pair of scissors. She cuts off my clothes and throws the cut garment pieces onto the floor.*

*She looks down between my legs.*

*"She's fully dilated. Get her into the delivery room."*

*The pain is overpowering. I feel like I might pass out.*

*The midwife is telling me to push.*

*I try to tell her that I am pushing but the words won't appear.*

*She says I must push harder.*

*And then the miracle happens.*

*Our daughter comes kicking and fighting into the world.*

*I'm holding Kelly in my arms. I'm crying*
*Not snow nor pain and suffering can take away the joy of this moment.*

I reach for the phone.
*How I love you, Kelly.*

# CHAPTER 14

It's getting late. Both Ives and Lesley are still at Lions Yard police station.

Lesley comes into Ives' office with that *just wait 'til you hear this* look on her face.

Ives yawns and looks up. "What do you have, June?"

She sits opposite him and places two printouts on the desktop. She shows him the first one. "We already have the test results from Westminster Morgue. DNA analysis of swabs taken by Julienne when she examined Aspinal's body."

Ives gives the results a cursory look. "So, what's new?"

Lesley smiles. "I thought I'd run a check on the results of the swabs taken by Isobel Cunningham's doctor after the rape."

"Why would you do that?"

"Bear with me, Steve." She shows him the second report. "There's a match between the DNA taken from Aspinal and that found on Cunningham."

"Aspinal raped Cunningham?"

"That's ninety-nine-point-nine per cent certain."

Ives looks to the ceiling. "You're going to tell me that changes everything."

"Well, you're always saying that in our line of work there's no such thing as coincidence."

Ives smiles as he hears his own words coming back at him. "OK. All along, I should have been taking my own advice, is that it?"

"In this case, that's a *yes*."

"So, where next?"

"The security footage from Ardensis. It's just come in."

# CHAPTER 15

*I'm smoothing out the picnic blanket, getting the lunch ready. The sun is shining. We're happy.*

*Here comes Kelly, her hair in curls. Smiling.*

*"Can I have strawberries, Mommy?"*

*I pretend to frown. "Oh, I don't know if we remembered them, darling. Let me see."*

*I'm making a show of searching the picnic basket and finding nothing more there. "Oh dear, it seems we're fresh out of strawberries."*

*Kelly looks forlorn.*

*John comes up beside me. "Your mother is such a tease."*

*He reaches into the basket and pulls out the punnet. "What do we have here? Strawberries. I put them in myself."*

*Kelly whoops with pleasure.*

*I'm laughing and pushing a plate of plump, ripe strawberries Kelly's way. "Your father's right. I am a teaser. How could we ever deny you anything, my love?"*

The scene fades. The sunlight is gone. Replaced by a terrible darkness.

A feeling of foreboding I can't shake off.

I pull the sheet over my head. The distant rattle and hum of the hospital beyond the room is sounding ever more alien. I want it to go away.

*I'm in the kitchen of a country cottage. My home.*

*Making breakfast for my daughter, Kelly. Beautiful twelve-year-old Kelly. She's complaining.*

*"Mom, I don't want to go today."*

*I'm replying. "But Kelly, you know you have to go to school."*

*"Just one day off."*

*"You know that would get me into trouble. It's the law. I have to send you."*

*I'm pausing to wipe a strand of blonde hair from her face. "Anyway, just think of all the things you'll miss if you don't go, and all the friends there you'll get to see."*

*Kelly is pushing the cereal bowl away. "I don't want to walk along the road. It's too dangerous. The traffic is going much too fast."*

*I'm acting as though this is not the most terrible moment in my life. The moment when I think she's inventing excuses for not going to school. "You don't mean that, Kelly. The road is well lit. It's only a few hundred yards to the school bus. There isn't some problem you're not telling me about, is there? You're not being bullied?"*

*"No, nothing like that."*

*"Then be a good girl. Don't let me down."*

*She's looking back at me with pleading eyes. "Then at least walk me to the bus."*

*"I don't have time, darling. You know I have to get the house ready for an important visitor your father wants to bring home from work tonight."*

*"OK, Mom."*

I sit bolt upright in the bed. I don't want to see what's coming next. I try to shut out the vision, to send it back with all the other unwanted memories that are locked away in the past, but this will not be.

*I'm looking down at the crumpled body of Kelly lying broken at the side of the road, just fifty yards from our house. Watching the life drain from her, long before the ambulance arrives.*

I reach for the phone.

*Kelly, can you ever forgive me?*

# CHAPTER 16

Ives and Lesley pick up coffee from the machine and settle down to look over the security camera footage from Ardensis.

Ives selects the fast playback option and they watch as events in the Ardensis entrance hall on the eve of Valentine's Day speed through. "Nothing unexpected so far, June. It's seven thirty and everyone's going home. There's Aspinal leaving."

He stops the playback at 11.15 PM. "But what's this? Mike Aspinal coming back into the office. And who's that with him?"

Lesley looks hard and long at the screen. "That's Isobel Cunningham. Judging from the photo given us by Ardensis personnel."

Ives restarts the playback. "They're side by side, if not exactly arm in arm. And by the look of them, I'd say they've been drinking."

They watch as the couple enter the lift together. "Safe to assume they went up to Aspinal's office?"

"There's no security footage of the upper floors, Steve, but I'd say that's right."

Ives puts the replay into reverse.

Lesley frowns. What are you looking for, Steve?"

"Just checking that we know the time that Cunningham left the building at going home time."

He stops the playback at 7.15 PM. "Ah, there she is. Leaving. About fifteen minutes before Aspinal. The sort of thing she'd do if she didn't want anyone to know she was going to meet up with him later." He puts the playback into fast forward and waits for it to return to 11.15 PM, when he pauses the action once more. "So, what do we know?"

"That Aspinal and Cunningham were together shortly before Aspinal's death. And that Aspinal was responsible for the sex attack she suffered."

"So, it's more than a working assumption to say that what we're looking at is the lead up to both the rape and Aspinal's death?"

"Let's call it a pretty safe bet."

Ives pauses to take a sip of coffee. "Do we know where Aspinal went after he left the Agency? Before returning to the office with Cunningham?"

"We do. Number plate recognition in Central London places Aspinal's Ferrari in a multi-storey car park in Soho." She calls up security camera footage on her laptop. "And, look what we have here. Aspinal and Cunningham walking side by side along Dean Street."

"So, they met and went drinking in a bar in Soho before coming back to the office?"

Lesley nods. "I'd say that's fair enough."

Ives looks back at the paused action on his screen that shows the couple entering the lift at Ardensis. "And though Aspinal raped her, I'd say from what we can see here, it looks like this started out with consent."

"And if that's so, something must have happened to turn that into rape."

"Like she said *no*"

"So, why did she say *no?*"

Ives speeds the playback on. Nothing changes in the empty entrance hall until 1.30 AM.

"There's Cunningham leaving. The way she looks around makes her seem furtive."

"You can't be sure of that."

"OK. So check the times. They arrive at 11.15 PM. Cunningham leaves at 1.30 AM. That's over two hours. And you know what that means?"

Lesley is there before him. "This places Isobel Cunningham at the murder scene within the time window identified by Julienne."

Ives gives a knowing smile. "So, we need to talk to her."

# CHAPTER 17

I wipe the tears from my eyes as another vision of the shattered fragments of what used to be invades my thoughts.

*Here's John, my husband, the one who loved me and who loves me no more. His eyes are red with tears. He's asking for an explanation, and the means of coming to terms with our loss.*

*I'm crying too. "It's my fault John. Kelly told me she didn't want to go. I made her leave. Can you ever forgive me?"*

The vision shifts. I fear I won't see him again.

*But here he is. And he looks as sad as a man can be.*

*He's telling me we can't go on. This marriage isn't working now that Kelly is gone.*

*"I've tried, Issy, I really have. But the pain of being here is too great. Every time I look at you I see Kelly. It reminds me of how beautiful and how full of life she was and how we've lost her."*

*"You're still blaming me. For sending her out that day. For not walking her to the bus and making sure she stayed safe."*

*"You know I wouldn't do that, Issy."*

*I'm in tears. "Admit it. You blame me. You still blame me. Don't you think I've tried and tried to find a way to turn back time to that day and do everything different? But it can't all be different, John. What's done is done. We need to stay together, from Kelly's sake."*

*He's holding my hand for the last time. "I can't, Issy. I've tried. I don't blame you. I blame myself. But that's not enough. Nothing's going to bring her back."*

When I stop crying, I wipe away fresh tears and make a note on the phone.

*I know I won't see John again.*

# CHAPTER 18

Ives and Lesley arrive at King's College Hospital, are shown to an empty waiting room and asked to wait for Mr Mortimer.

When the harassed-looking doctor appears it's clear he's been called away from his rounds.

Ives takes the lead in apologizing. "I'm sorry to disturb you, doctor. We need permission to interview Isobel Cunningham."

Mortimer shakes his head. "I have to say, it's too early. She's recovering well and is responding much better than when she was brought in. But she remains fragile."

"She still has problems after what happened to her?"

"Yes. She's in a state of shock. She has memory problems, too, maybe triggered by the attack. It confirms much of what her GP diagnosed. So far, progress is as expected. There are signs of a significant recovery in mental function and that should improve with every hour that passes. But she's starting from a very low base."

"But she should be able to answer a few questions."

"Again, yes, that might be possible. But for her peace of mind, I'd be much happier if you could give her a few days."

Ives lowers his voice. "We wouldn't want to trouble her at this time, doctor, but we're investigating a murder and, I hope you'll appreciate, we need to make progress."

Mortimer doesn't relent. "I'm sorry. I have to forbid it. You must wait at least twenty four hours." He pauses. "Now, I must be getting back to my other patients."

As they leave, Ives can't hide his rage at being turned away like this. "Doctors. Think they rule the place."

Lesley tries to calm him. "Just a reminder, Steve. This is a hospital. And here, they do."

"OK. OK. I get it. We can't see her but, if we get a warrant, no one can stop us searching her workspace and her apartment."

"I'll get onto it first thing in the morning, Steve."

# CHAPTER 19

Nurse Hewitt comes in and takes my blood pressure and pulse rate.

I'm trying to work out what's happening. "Why this?"

She enters the readings on the chart at the foot of the bed. "Mr Mortimer has asked us to check every three hours."

"Mortimer?"

"Your consultant. He's going to see to it that you'll soon be better."

She hands me a cup of water and places a stainless steel tray before me. Two green coloured tablets sit on the tray.

"Mr Mortimer wants you to take these."

I swallow the pills.

"What are they for?"

"They'll help you sleep."

She tidies the bedclothes and sees that I'm comfortable before she leaves.

The ghosts of memory return as I close my eyes.

*I'm looking down on Kelly. Looking into her frightened, pleading eyes.*
*Watching the spirit of her life leave her.*
*Seeing myself lost and alone on that cold, November roadside.*

The vision fades.

I feel the call of sleep, a call I can no longer resist.

My last thoughts.

*I will remember. No matter how painful, I will remember it all.*

# DAY 2

# CHAPTER 20

A male nurse stands over me and brushes a moist wipe across my forehead. "Good morning, Mrs Cunningham."

I'm coming round from deep, deep sleep. "Where is Nurse Hewitt?"

"She's off duty today. My name is Phil. Nurse Phil Wetherby. I'll be looking after you."

"What time is it?"

"It's 6.00 AM. That's when the morning starts here."

"And where is here?"

"The Haven at King's College Hospital. You're safe here."

His words wake up the ghosts within me. Yes, they've been sleeping, too. I realise I must have been dreaming. I can feel the echoes of their incessant quest to make them known to me. But now that I'm awake, they've left no trace other than the knowledge that they were there. And the yesterday they've left behind feels like it was filled with pain. It's here with me. I recall being there.

"Mr Mortimer?"

"He'll be on his ward rounds later this morning. He'll see you then. In the meantime, don't worry, keep comfortable."

He takes my temperature and blood pressure and adds the details to the chart clipped to the end of the bed. "There. Everything in order."

I find the phone and stare at the notes there.

*Why did Colin need my help?*

*Mary is a good friend.*

*I should have trusted my mother.*
*John, how did I ever lose you?*
*Mike is dead.*
*Why do I feel so guilty?*
*Colin behaves like he owes me.*
*How I love you, Kelly.*
*Kelly, can you ever forgive me?*
*I know I won't see John again.*

Is this me? Am I the one who wrote these words?

It must be me. Why else would I have this?

I know I have to come to terms with what I can see here.

I have to let those ghosts of yesterday in once more. Let them dance and run their crazy patterns in my mind.

# CHAPTER 21

Ives arrives at Lions Yard station early and finds Lesley waiting with two cups of coffee.

He takes his cup from the tray and sits opposite her. "It's not even 7 AM."

Lesley takes the remaining cup. "Been here since six. Looking over the analysis reports."

"Anything new?"

"Well, it's Mike Aspinal's semen on the swab taken from Issy Cunningham. And there's a straight match with the DNA taken from him in the morgue by Julienne. There's no doubt about that."

"So, we know that Aspinal raped her. And the rape happened when they returned to the Agency. What's the problem?"

"Though you haven't come out and said as much, I can tell you think she killed him."

"What's wrong with that? She's angry at what he's done. She strikes back. We can place her with certainty at the murder scene and at the time of the murder. What more do you want?"

"It still doesn't mean she did it."

"Why do you say that?"

"When Cunningham was examined at the hospital, she'd been violently attacked. Molested. In shock. Traumatised by what Aspinal did to her."

"OK, she hates him. She has cause."

"Julienne tells us that Aspinal was killed by lethal injection."

"So?"

"So, despite Cunningham being traumatized, that physically damaged, before she leaves the building she manages to somehow source potassium chloride and some method of administering it. I don't think so. That's no spur of the moment thing."

Ives scratches his head. "I can't say I like it, but I see what you're getting at. So, where does that leave us? We need more evidence."

"We have the Aspinal computer from Ardensis. We need Cunningham's. We also need her phone and search records. The technical boys are already working on Aspinal's computer and I have orders out with the Internet service providers."

"But we're missing something here, June. We need to search Cunningham's work space."

Lesley waves a computer printout at him. "We have confirmation of the warrant to search Cunningham's apartment."

OK, let's check them out. The apartment first and then Cunningham's possessions at Ardensis."

# CHAPTER 22

I find myself staring at the phone again. I'm trying to stay away from all I might find there but the soft glow draws me back in.

Here's the image of a man with piercing grey eyes and raven black hair with the name Michael Aspinal beside it.

My palms begin to sweat and I begin to feel nauseous.

I know him. He's one who died. Called himself Mike, not Michael. I think he did me harm. And it was all my fault.

I read through the messages next to Michael Aspinal's name. One stands out.

*Come to my office at 6.00 PM and we can talk about it again then.*

*I can see the door. The door to his office. I hear my footsteps as I approach. I feel sick in my stomach, dry in my throat. The impulse that I should be running away when all the time there's this voice inside compelling me to go on. Here I am, reaching forward, gripping the door handle, pressing down, hearing the catch slip as the door opens.*

The splinter of memory fades and I'm back in this darkest of places, hoping that none of this will return. I want it to go away.

But it comes again. In detail. So much detail.

Once it starts, it won't stop.

*I'm back there. I'm looking down, seeing my hand as I push open the door to Mike Aspinal's office.*

*He looks up. "Issy, to what do I owe the pleasure?"*

*I'm trying to make this appear as casual as I can. "I'd like your help, Mike."*

He's giving me a self-satisfied smile. *"That's what I'm here for. I work hard to be approachable, not aloof like Vince."*

I try to turn this into a compliment that doesn't sound neither too ingratiating nor too cynical. *"You've been a breath of fresh air since you took over, Mike. And that's why I'm here. Now that the agency is more open, more responsive."*

*"Exactly as I want it to be. How can I help?"*

I come out with it. *"I don't think it's a good idea to dismiss Colin."*

*"You know about that?"*

*"He told me you were going to announce his dismissal in the morning."*

*"And he asked you to come here and plead his case? A woman to do a man's work? Why does he think you can say anything he can't say himself?"*

*"Because it takes a woman to let you know what a tragedy this would be for Colin's family. And because I know you're a reasonable, fair-minded man who wouldn't want to see an injustice done."*

*"So, you're here to talk justice, are you, Isobel?"*

*"I'm here to convince you."*

He moves closer.

I don't move away. Is this the beginning of it all? Is this what leads to how I'm feeling now?

He continues. *"He broke the rules. What else can I do? There are standards that have to be maintained. For the benefit of everyone. The agency. For us all."*

*"I understand you have to enforce rules. But surely it's not right to do that without looking at the consequences."*

He interrupts. *"And I do. But I have a moral responsibility. Not just to myself but to everyone here."*

*"But don't you see that if every time someone steps out of line the roof falls in on them, there will never be justice in anything we do?"*

*"That's all very utopian, Isobel. And it would all make perfect sense if the world were a better place and we had time to understand how and why people do the things they do. How they could become better people. But business doesn't work that way. Running a company means taking tough decisions. You think I like it? Of course not. But it comes with the turf."*

*"Dismissing Colin will ruin him and his family."*

*"There are other places to work. He isn't the first person to lose a job and he won't be the last. If he has fight in him, he'll get through this."*

*"Not if you won't give him a reference."*

*"He told you that?"*

*"Is it true?"*

*He moves even closer and places his hand on my arm. I don't pull away. I know I should.*

*It's a mistake to try to use my femininity to try to change his mind. I know that I shouldn't be doing this. But I don't move away.*

*His voice is quieter.* "It's not that I don't want Colin to have another chance. But you see where this would leave me don't you? I'm dismissing him for a gross misdemeanour and yet I'm writing him a glowing reference letter saying he's the best employee in the world. That would be improper. That would be morally irresponsible. If anyone asks me that's what I'm going to have to say. That he's behaved badly and placed the agency at risk. So, I can't write the letter."

"Most do."

"Well, I can't."

*I allow him to move even closer so that I can feel his breath on my face.*

*What am I doing here? Why do I believe I can convince him when everything he's doing and saying is pointing to the inevitable conclusion that this man is never going to be persuaded by a rational argument about what's right and wrong? Yet I can't stop myself from trying.*

*If I pull away, set some distance between us, he'll get a different kind of message. But I'm not doing that.*

"Then all I can do is appeal to your humanity, Mike. The decision may be right but the result will be out of all proportion. Find a way to keep him here. Discipline him, yes, and then make sure he never does anything as stupid again. But don't destroy his life."

*He's touching my hair.* "Maybe there is a way, after all."

"What do you mean?"

"I've always had a thing for you, Issy, you must know that. You're so reserved and so aloof from all the cut and thrust of what's going on all around you, so concerned to find a logical reason for everything, and that's something I find attractive. Like you're my other half. My flip side. We'd make a great team. Help me discover how far we can go with this and I'll see what I can do to take your advice on what to do with Colin."

*Now, too late, I draw back.* "I didn't mean to give you any impression of that kind."

*He bares his teeth.* "Then, let's call this what it is, plain and simple. Sleep with me and I won't dismiss Colin."

*I'm pulling away from him and running towards the door.*

*He calls after me.* "I'll give you twenty-four hours to change your mind. Twenty-four hours and that's it."

*Mike. Someone I should never have trusted to keep his word.*

My body starts to tremble. It begins in my legs and arms and spreads like a wave to my abdomen and then to my chest and on up to my neck and face until I lie here sobbing, alone in the silence of the hospital room.

I should never have allowed myself to be that close to him. Never given any impression like that.

When the sobbing stops, I make a note on the phone.

*I know why I hate Mike.*

# CHAPTER 23

Ives and Lesley arrive at Bentham Gardens and press the entry call button.

As they wait for a response, Ives can't help a stray comment. "You know, June, back in Victorian times this place was a mission for fallen women. And from what I hear, there were quite a few of them round these parts back then."

Lesley doesn't rise to the bait. "So I guess that explains why we're now standing beneath a large stained glass window of a rainbow that says in large white lettering: *Westminster Mission*."

"All right. You're unimpressed. No change there, then." He carries on. "I got a call to this place a few months back. What remains of the mission is really just a shell. They've shoehorned in eighty or so apartments on the site, most used as hotel lets by the holding company and a few used by long term owner occupiers."

After three attempts to call someone, the door clicks open and they enter the lobby.

At the entrance desk a beehive-haired receptionist is dealing with a French couple that are checking in. Some sort of argument is going on about the room rate.

Ives has no time to wait. He approaches the desk and shows his Police ID. "I have a warrant to search number twenty-one."

The receptionist doesn't blink. "I'll just complete my work with these guests."

Ives bangs his fist on the counter. "You'll stop what you're doing and listen carefully to what I'm going to tell you."

The French couple draw back, a look of shock on their faces.

Ives presses on. "Obstructing the police is a serious offence."

The receptionist makes a great show of apologizing to the French tourists before returning her attention to Ives. "Number twenty-one. That's Ms Cunningham's apartment."

"That's right. I need you to show us up there."

Without saying anything more, she shows Ives and Lesley to the lift. On the second floor she leads them along the walkway to apartment twenty-one and lets them in.

Ives dismisses her. "There. That wasn't so difficult, was it? You can check in your guests now. We'll let you know when we're finished."

The apartment is spacious by London standards, with high ceilings inherited from what remained of the Victorian parts of the complex.

Lesley looks around. "Two bedrooms and integrated kitchen cum diner. I'll take the bedrooms."

They both pull on protective gloves.

Lesley finds a desk with a laptop computer in the nearest bedroom. She searches the desk drawers and finds nothing of interest. She makes a mental note to remove the computer for investigation back at Lions Yard. When she completes her search of the second bedroom and finds nothing of interest there, she returns to the kitchen diner.

Ives has completed his search.

"Thought there was nothing but the usual stuff here. Until I found this." He holds out a photograph. "Take a look."

Lesley inspects it. "It's Cunningham with a child. It's signed *I love you Mummy XXX*. Must be her own child."

"Surprising. Didn't Marianne French tell us that Cunningham was a loner, with no children?"

"Where did you find it?"

"Amongst a pile of letters and junk mail." He pauses. "Why was this something she wanted to hide? Why not have a photo like this in a frame on the wall like anyone else?"

They bag the evidence.

Ives picks up the computer and carries it back to the lift.

Back at the entrance hallway, the receptionist is still arguing with the French tourists.

Ives gives a wave as they go past. "You can close up number twenty-one now. We have what we came for."

# CHAPTER 24

Justin Hardman looks at himself in the mirror as he shaves. He likes what he sees. A man approaching forty but with the bright-eyed zeal of a twenty-year-old. A man in control.

He knows where he stands in this troubled world. He despises those who don't have money and make an issue of being poor. Half of society feeds off their incompetence. Yet he hates even more those who are wealthy and pretend to help those on whose backs their money is made. He admires the charity CEOs who pay themselves six figure salaries. At least they're honest enough to admit they are running a real, profit making business. He would never support the hypocrites who say they are skimming from the poor. The poor deserve all they get. What matters is being honest about the realities of this life.

When he needs money, he knows where to get it and how to get it. Because he knows what money is and how the wealth that comes with it was created.

He knows about his distant family ancestors who owned slaves working on the sugar plantations of Trinidad, those who were compensated well for the loss of their human property when slavery was abolished. He knows that the work of those slaves, whipped until bleeding as often as not in the treadmills used to process tobacco or sugar, lives on in the money that changes hands today. The indelible mark of his family is still on it. He knows that those who cannot face up to such truths about where their money comes from do not deserve to keep it.

He knows of those other family ancestors who benefited from the rape of Africa, profiting from the shipping companies that transported slaves and returned with tobacco and cotton from the New World. And he knows of the smarter branches of the family who distanced themselves from the brutality of the trade by profiting even further from the import and export duties levied on each shipment that came in or out of London, Liverpool or Bristol, while all the time showing an exemplary face to those around them, priding themselves on the donations they made to the fine buildings that still grace those cities.

Yes, it's the wealth created by his ancestors and those like them that still flows as a flood tide of ever increasing strength through today's London.

And he knows of those later family ancestors whose crimes, though vile and treacherous to many, were so long concealed by the passage of time that they were able to pass themselves off as altruistic patrons of the arts without risk of ridicule. The spoils of their dreadful deeds circulate still.

Yes, he knows his true place in this great scheme of things. What does it matter if in this generation he was born with none of the advantages he might have expected had his recent family not contrived to squander these fruits of the past long before he could inherit them? Unlike those around him who took entitlement for granted, he hadn't been to a good school nor sent on to a place kept waiting for him at Oxbridge.

The only advantage Justin Hardman inherited was an insatiable ambition to succeed by any means possible and an unstoppable desire to recover what is owed from the past. And he knows this matters more than any accident of birth. His is the stronger form of entitlement. The wealth that should be his, the dead labour that has been passed down through the ages, might be now in the hands of others but it is still rightfully his. It is only appropriate that he must do all he can to now take it back.

He washes and dries his face and chooses his clothes for the day from the walk-in dressing room nearby. The choice of over twenty designer Italian suits and over a hundred handmade shirts would overwhelm some. But he knows he has style and can let instinct make the selection. The steel-grey suit. The blue-check shirt.

This is the most important thing he's learned. The appearance of wealth attracts more wealth. That's how to stay ahead in this life and get even. Something his father had never understood when he told his son he'd never make anything of himself. If his father could see him now. But he couldn't. His father had died a loser.

Hardman walks to the breakfast place near Borough Market, picking his way through the traders setting up their stalls for the day. He likes the smells and the colours of the place almost as much as he likes the sight of others working hard as he breezes by.

This place is like him. Defined by its past yet confident in its future. Since the Romans, generation on generation has been here, living out the daily struggle of existence, winning and losing, determined to fight it out, just as his family has lived out its own struggle, winning and losing, as determined as this place itself to survive. More than surviving. Emerging battered and bruised from the past yet back on the rise, vibrant now, ready to take on the world. Claiming back all it is rightly owed.

Inside the *Blue Oyster*, as on every morning, he orders breakfast – today, coffee with scrambled eggs and mushrooms.

It's unlike Frank Taylor to be late. They meet here at this time each day. This is their office. People looking on might see Frank as some sort of employee or, since they could not be aware of Hardman's heterosexual preferences, as some kind of lover. Frank is none of these things. He's a protector and an enforcer. A partner who is essential to Hardman's business.

There is no need to let people know about Frank's abilities. If his scarred and craggy face doesn't serve as a warning, his reputation alone is enough in this part of the world. Convictions for grievous bodily harm and manslaughter are just the acknowledged extent of his impulse to violence. Word-of-mouth spreads far beyond the East End the lurid details of the beatings and tortures he hands out when his polite requests for compliance are turned down.

Before Hardman took him on board, Frank Taylor's rage was without real purpose. Now, together, it is focused and they both prosper.

Breakfast would be some time yet in coming and Frank is late. This is wasting time. The thing Hardman hates more than anything else.

He takes out his phone and dials.

When Frank Taylor picks up, he is full of apologies. "Sorry, Justin. I had a busy night and the traffic is mental."

"OK Frank. I'm in the Oyster as usual. We need to talk about what needs to be done about Jarrett."

"You're saying he's not listening again?"

"Time to remind him how much he cares about his daughter."

"Leave it to me, Justin. I'll have a word with him before I come over to you."

# CHAPTER 25

I toss and turn in the hospital bed.

The ghosts of memory, messengers of my guilt, are coming closer now. With every passing minute, it's becoming ever more difficult to stop them. Yet I fear that as soon as they arrive, they'll be gone and I'll be returned to the emptiness of this darkest of dark places. Yet, while they are here, they take over my whole being.

*I'm with Colin. In his office with the door closed so no one can hear.*

*He's looking at me with wide open, pleading eyes. "Well, how did it go with Mike? From the way you look, I'd say not too well."*

*I can feel the tension in my stomach that tells me how difficult this is. "I don't know how to tell you this, Colin."*

*"What did he say? Is he willing to reconsider?"*

*I nod. "Yes."*

*"Thank you! You don't know how much this means to me. And Angie and the kids."*

*"It's not what you think. He wants me to sleep with him."*

*Colin blinks a dozen times before he can reply. "Did I hear that right?"*

*"He wants sex in exchange for not giving you a reprimand."*

*"I don't believe you, Issy. Even he couldn't be that shallow. Ever since he's been in charge he's behaved like a paragon of virtue. Enforcing to the letter every regulation he can find, and where he can't find any, making more up. All in the name of doing things properly, of enforcing what he takes to be some kind of innate justice in following the rules. And now he's saying he wants to do that for everyone except himself?"*

*"I guess he thinks that's what having power is all about." I pause. "Just what did you do, Colin?"*

*"I told you. We lost the Forerunner Technology account. Mike won't believe me when I tell him I had nothing to do with that. He's saying I did it deliberately."*

*"Well, did you?"*

*"No. But that doesn't really matter. It's what Mike thinks and he's certain I'm to blame."*

*Colin gets up from his chair and holds both of my hands, just as a brother would. "I don't know how I could ask you this. Are you sure that Mike was serious in what he was saying?"*

*I nod. "Yes, he was quite serious."*

*"And he would go ahead and fire me if you didn't?"*

*"That's what he said."*

*He's on the point of breaking into tears. "You know how my family will be hurt if I lose this job, Issy. What I didn't tell you is that Angie has complications. Her eyes. She may well lose her sight. I don't have to tell you what this means for the family. And without this job we'll certainly lose the house. The kids won't be able to stay at their current school. Our lives will never be the same."*

*I interrupt him. "I can't, Colin."*

*"Please, I'm begging you."*

I sit up in the bed. The memory fades.

I pull out the phone.

*Is Colin holding back on me?*

# CHAPTER 26

Driving Ives, Lesley finds a route to Old Street avoiding much of the traffic. Once they arrive at Ardensis, they are shown to Marianne French's office.

Ives gives her a reassuring look. "You're in charge now?"

There is no doubting the irony in her voice as she replies. "I'd be the last to say there was anything like a glass ceiling in this company. But someone has to fill in now Vince Blakemore is still away and Mike Aspinal is no longer with us. And that someone is me."

"You've managed to reach Blakemore?"

She nods. "He's as shocked as we all are. He's boarding a 'plane as we speak. Should be with us sometime tomorrow."

"We'll need to speak to him." Ives pauses. "Meanwhile, we'd like to search Mrs Cunningham's work space."

Marianne French shows them to Issy Cunningham's desk.

Ives pulls on surgical gloves and opens each desk drawer in turn but can find nothing that alerts him. There's nothing but the expected office dross.

He's about to call it a day when he notices something. "The bottom drawer looks a place to hide something."

Lesley doesn't understand. "What do you mean, Steve?"

He lifts out the segmented file separator with its collection of papers and letters and places the assembly on the desktop.

What remains in the bottom of the drawer is a cloth bag with a drawstring tied in a bow. "Now, why would this be here?"

He pulls open the drawstring and shakes the contents out onto the desktop.

There is a syringe and a plastic screw top bottle containing a colourless liquid.

"Can't believe we almost missed this." He pauses. "Bag the evidence, June. Get Julienne onto it."

"Yes, Steve."

"And don't try to tell me this isn't what was used to kill Mike Aspinal."

# CHAPTER 27

Frank Taylor parks his car at the end of Rushworth Street and walks to the apartment building. Better to surprise Jarrett, who would only try to barricade himself inside if he knew what was coming.

Jarrett is on the top floor. Taylor grunts as he begins to climb the stairs.

Why is Stan Jarrett causing so much trouble? He must know that the lease on the building has been taken over by the French holding company and that they have plans to create luxury apartments here. He must know it's time to leave, that the company has other ideas about this run down place.

One by one the other residents have moved out. The sensible ones have taken the sweeteners offered by Justin Hardman. The more resistant have required a little more persuading by Taylor himself. Now only Jarrett remains and he's holding up the whole project. He needs to wise up and understand that there's no longer room for people like him in London. There's plenty of space out in Essex where all the others like him are now going.

It's no use being sentimental about it, Taylor knows that. The old East End communities have come and gone. The tough men and the wily women who raised their families in the shadow of the Empire were a force to reckon with and produced men like Taylor himself. But that's all in the past. There's no point romanticizing the men of reputation who ruled these places, no point trying to make heroes out of villains. Today is today and has to be accepted for what it is. Taylor knows how to move on.

He reaches the top of the stairs and is breathless. Perhaps the years are catching up on him. He takes a moment to fill his lungs with air before knocking at Jarrett's door.

The door opens a crack for someone to try to work out who is there. Taylor shoulders his way in.

"Thanks for letting me in, Stan. You and me need a little talk."

Jarrett's teeth are chattering. "I'm sorry, Mr Taylor. I didn't mean anything by trying to close the door."

Taylor smiles. "Just a friendly word, Stan, that's all." He pauses to make sure that he's being listened to. "You do realise, don't you, that this can't go on."

"They put the rent up to double what it was but I'm paying it. What more do you want me to do?"

"Hasn't the penny dropped yet, son. You and your family. You're the last ones here. Everyone else has left. Don't you think there's a message somewhere in that?"

"We're paying the rent. We have every right to be here."

"So, where's that money coming from, Stan? Doesn't look to me like you have two pennies to rub together and yet you've kept paying." Taylor looks at his man with a menacing stare. "Someone wants this place. You're in the way."

Jarrett doesn't look like he's about to see sense anytime soon. "I can't help that. I've got a family to care for. They come first. Anyone could understand that."

Taylor smiles. "Your daughter. Her name's Emily, isn't it, Stan? What is she? Sixteen now? Going on seventeen? Starting to see boys. A difficult time for any father."

"Leave her out of this."

"I'm not sure I can, Stan. Wouldn't take much for things to get out of hand with the boys now, would it? I hear she's an attractive girl."

"What are you saying?"

"Just that I know a bunch of lads who wouldn't mind getting masked up and getting some of that. You know, Emily's on her way home from school and before she can get here she's pushed into an alley and four or five of my young acquaintances give her a good seeing to. Kind of event that a young girl might never recover from. Most likely blight the rest of her life."

Jarrett is trying to look angry. "You can't treat her like that. I'll…."

Taylor reaches down and grabs Jarrett's testicles with a giant hand. "Or you'll go to the police? Or have one of the liberal minded lawyer friends who've been encouraging you to stay here try to interfere? I don't think so. First you'd have to let them know where you've been getting the money to pay to stay in this place. Then you'd have to face a life as the man who grassed up Frank Taylor. No one grasses Frank Taylor. And, in any case, you know there's no way the police will be able to connect what happens to Emily to me."

Jarrett's face contorts in agony and is on the point of turning blue before Taylor releases his grip.

"Let's see sense, Stan. Save yourself. Save your family. Save young Emily from having to go through all that."

Jarrett fights for breath. "OK, Mr Taylor. We'll leave."

"You've got twenty-four hours. If you're still here after that your world will start to fall apart."

Taylor lets himself out. He feels no guilt about threatening the man's child. Whatever works. That's all that matters.

When he reaches the car, he calls Justin Hardman who picks up straight away.

"Justin. Jarrett will be out of there today."

Hardman sounds pleased. "Good work, Frank. I knew I could count on you. Remind me to increase your cut. See you at the Oyster."

"I'm on my way there right now."

As he drives away, Frank Taylor can't help thinking about just how much Justin stands to gain from handing over the apartment block ready for development. Perhaps it's as much as half a million. Frank could expect ten per cent of that. Not bad for a morning's work.

# CHAPTER 28

Colin Tempest feels nervous as he enters the Board Room at Ardensis. He's last on the list to be interviewed by DI Ives. There's only one way to think about this. It must be routine. They need to question everyone, don't they? So, why have they insisted he come in from home? Time to hide those nerves.

The Inspector begins. The short woman beside him, who is introduced as DS Lesley, takes notes. "Tell me, Colin, what do you think of Mike Aspinal?"

"I would never speak ill of the dead."

Ives smiles. "OK. Beyond that, how would you say he ran the office?"

Colin shuffles in his seat. "He was doing his job, that's all. Not everyone saw it the way he did but that's business. You don't get to choose who you work with."

"So, you didn't like him?"

"I didn't say that"

"But you implied it."

"OK if I didn't. Truth is, no one liked him. You must be aware of that by now."

"Because of the way he treated people?"

"Yes."

"And how did he treat you?"

"As badly as everyone else."

"So, there was animosity between him and you?"

"No. As I said, it was business. If we had our ups and downs it was because of business."

"So, there were issues between you. Do you mind telling me what they were?"

"It's no secret. He threatened to sack me."

"What for?"

"Some rule of his that I'd broken." Colin shuffles in his seat once more. "You don't need the details. It was a business deal that we disagreed on."

"What deal?"

"We have a client. Forerunner Technology. They've developed an algorithm that they claim can interpret personal data in a new way. I told Mike that the technology didn't work and that the company would fail, so it wouldn't do our reputation any good if we took them as a client. Mike accused me of deliberately losing the contract."

"So, where were you at midnight on Valentine's Day morning?"

"At home."

"Alone?"

"Yes. I'm living alone. Is that a crime?"

Ives waits for Lesley to complete her note taking. "So, tell me about Issy Cunningham. How are you involved with her?"

"I wouldn't say we were *involved*. We're work colleagues. Nothing more. Nothing less."

"You're sure you don't want to add to that?"

"No. We just have a normal working relationship. "How would you describe her relationship with Mike Aspinal?"

"That was between him and her."

"You wouldn't care to elaborate?"

"Again, I wouldn't call it any kind of *relationship*. He fancied her, all right. You could tell that from the way he looked at her. But as far as I know, that's all there was to it."

"You wouldn't say she was the kind to lead him on?"

"She's not the type."

"You know he was the perpetrator of the sex attack on her?"

Colin feels the tension rising from his stomach, threatening to take his breath away. "I didn't know that."

"And it shakes you up, hearing that?"

"It does. It's nothing I would have expected."

Colin can't help thinking that the sole purpose of these questions is for the Inspector to observe his reactions. And that he's been doing a poor job of hiding his true feelings.

"We'll end it there, then. We'll need to speak with you again as the investigation proceeds."

# CHAPTER 29

I'm awake, dazzled by the glaring bright lighting of the hospital.

*My eyes are open and I can see him. Mike Aspinal, there right before me, opening the front passenger door of his Ferrari, patting my bottom as he ushers me into the seat.*

*"I'm glad you decided to come. I can promise you a great time."*

*I'm feeling sick to the pit of my stomach, knowing this is all wrong. Why am I agreeing to this? Is there no other way to save Colin and his family?*

*We're seated in the champagne bar in Soho, surrounded by the super wealthy, keen to show they've made it by throwing their money around. Everyone is smiling. I feel as cold as ice inside.*

*He's trying to give the impression that we're on a first date and I can tell from the way he's looking me up and down that he's imagining me with my clothes off, removing each garment one by one like a glutton weighing up his next meal.*

*He's touching my hair. "You know tomorrow is Valentine's Day. Why don't we bring the whole thing forward a day. Make like it's already started."*

*Now, we're back in his car. His driving is erratic, affected by the champagne. I'm hoping he'll be stopped for drink driving, to bring an end to this arrangement that never should have been. But there are no police in sight.*

*I could stop it right here but I don't. I tell myself that I'm doing the right thing, trying to break down the barriers between us so I can change his mind about Colin.*

*We're arriving back at the Agency. Going into his office.*

*I ask why here? He tells me everything is more important here.*

*He's smiling and pointing to the ice bucket beside the office couch. More champagne. He pours the drinks, offers me one.*

*He comes up close and places his hands on my shoulders. I can feel the strength in those hands. He's pushing me down onto the couch and telling me this is no time to change my mind.*

*I can smell him now he's this close to me. An expensive cologne. The kind, no doubt, he thinks will make him irresistible. Something he's paid plenty for, as if that would prove the point in itself. The kind of smell that fills my nostrils with loathing.*

*He whispers. "Like I told you, I've always wondered about you, Issy. Why so alone? Such a good-looking woman with no love life. We all need a love life, Issy. You know it's what makes half bearable the whole rotten world we've made for ourselves. Without it, where would we be?"*

*Now he's touching me and I can sense his arousal, the slight tremble of his hands as he begins to handle a prize he thinks he would never win. I feel like a commodity, a plaything to be placed in his mental trophy room alongside the flashy car, the expensive clothes and the other women he has no doubt taken in this way.*

*He starts to kiss me. Gentle at first. Then, when I don't respond, with increasing urgency.*

*I can't believe this is the man who parades his virtue in holding up the rules as something that no one should ever be allowed to break when all along he's preparing to violate me. I want to tell him what a hypocrite he is, but I doubt this will mean a thing to him. He's that shallow. He really does believe that the world is his and he can depose in any way he sees fit. Who's to stop him?*

*I push his hands away. "There's something I want to know, Mike. Why aren't you at all bothered by having one rule for yourself and one for everyone else?"*

*He gives a drunken smile. "What on earth do you mean, Issy?"*

*"The reason why you have me here."*

*The smile disappears. "It's just what it means to have power."*

*"And you don't care if the angels look down and weep?"*

*"There are no angels."*

*He pauses and I can see him weighing me up again, imagining the pleasure he is on the point of achieving. "So, why so serious? We're here to have some fun. An experience neither of us is ever going to forget."*

*He places his hand between my legs, pushing upwards.*

*I know that all along I never planned to go through with this. Somehow, I'd hoped to be able to make him see sense and change his mind about Colin, let me go, give up this blind exercise in power for the sake of it. But the chance has never come. He's been clever like that.*

*He presses me further down on the couch. I feel the weight of his body on top of me. I try to shout out but he has a hand across my mouth.*

*He's the one shouting now. "We're not here to discuss morality, Issy. We're here to enjoy each other. And I'm here to bring a little love back into your life."*

*I force his hand away. "I don't want this. Please stop."*

*"And what about Colin? What are you going to tell him when he hears he's out of a job?"*

*"You don't have to do that to him."*

*He snarls. "Listen, you stupid bitch, do you really think I was ever going to let him get away with what he's done?"*

This ghost of memory fades.

I sit up in the bed, my body shaking with remembered rage.

I reach for the phone and make a new message.

*Mike raped me.*

# CHAPTER 30

Back at Lions Yard, Ives finds DI Lesley working at one of the screens in the incident room.

"Tell me, June, what do we have from the technical boys on what they've found on Aspinal's computer?"

She stops what she's doing and swivels her seat to face him. "Their reports are slowly coming through. Nothing much yet. His social media accounts are full of the kind of stuff you might expect. Holidays in the sun, his car, photos of him with his dogs."

"Makes me wonder why so many people choose to spend so much of their time telling others what they do when anyone with a ha'penny of sense can see that not much of it's worth a tinker's cuss."

"As you might suppose, Steve. But it's the kind of stuff that keeps a billion or two people happy. Not much wrong with that. Any way, there is something of interest in Aspinal's output. There are no real friends. Male or female. Seems he was loner."

"So Aspinal is just an average guy?"

"Not quite. Outside of social media, there's significant use of dating sites and heavy use of adult sites."

"You mean porn?"

"Yes. Porn. But nothing gross."

"So, he is an ordinary Joe, then."

"Again, not quite. He started using a new messaging app a few weeks back. It's one of the ones we want regulated."

"You mean one that's heavily encrypted?"

"625 bit military strength. The tech boys say it's next to impossible to unscramble."

"So, we ask the operating company."

"They're out in Silicon Valley. They refuse all requests as a matter of course. Say it's a recipe for opening a back door in their system."

"So, we know he has something to hide but we won't get to know what it is unless we can find a way to de-encrypt it ourselves. Is that it?"

"That's pretty much it. Though we can deduce a few things."

"Such as?"

"Well, the number and frequency of the messages he sent spiked in the few days before his death. Just one or two messages a day in the previous five weeks. Then twenty the day before he died. As if he was heading for some kind of outcome."

"But we don't get to know what that was?"

"That's right. Without finding a way to unscramble those messages, we're going to have to discover that some other way."

"So, what do we have from the Cunningham machines?"

"We have the early analysis of Cunningham's phone records and computers. The technical boys made a chart of her contacts, with the more contacts made, the bigger the lettering. You know, one of those tag clouds. And one name stands out. Mary Duggan. Issy Cunningham's best friend at university."

"They've remained close, then?"

"They both studied Chemistry at University of London. Cunningham found her way into advertising. Mary Duggan stayed, became a lecturer there."

Ives' eyes light up. "So, we need talk to Mary Duggan. And dig into more background on Issy Cunningham before we set out."

# CHAPTER 31

By the time Frank Taylor arrives at the Blue Oyster, Justin Hardman has finished breakfast and is working at his laptop computer.

Taylor comes in and sits facing his boss. "Sorry I'm late, Justin. But I guess you're pleased that I cleared up our little problem with Jarrett. He won't give us any more trouble."

Hardman glances up from the computer screen. "Good to hear of the man's concern for the safety of his daughter. Makes you think those that say the world is going to hell in a handcart have it wrong after all."

Taylor looks perplexed.

Hardman smiles. "Never mind, Frank. Just something people say."

"What now?"

"Time to concentrate on what's happening at Ardensis. Now Aspinal's gone, someone owes us, and owes us big."

Hardman pulls out his phone and dials.

Marianne French picks up on the third ring. "I told you not to call me at the office."

"We need to talk."

"The police have been all over this place."

"Then tomorrow it is."

"OK. I'll come to the Blue Oyster."

"I'll be here until ten. Make sure you're here by then."

# CHAPTER 32

The journey to the Chemistry Department at University of London should take less than fifteen minutes, but here they are outside St Paul's, stuck in late afternoon traffic.

Ives is trying to remain positive and not think too much about the time they are losing as the vehicles ahead of them, mainly London Transport buses, show no sign of moving.

"June, you're sure we can't get to interview Issy Cunningham before late afternoon at the earliest?"

Lesley, who is driving, can afford to take her eyes off the road and look back at him. "'Fraid not Steve. When I called Mr Mortimer he was quite adamant. Not only would our visit alarm her, we wouldn't get much out of it. He said he'll revisit the situation as soon as he can."

"OK. Then take me through what we know about her so far."

"Well, the story that she's a loner doesn't add up. Had me fooled until we found the photograph of her with her daughter. Then I found that she's changed her name. Small, but significant. Isobel is her middle name. She used to go by the name Rachel Cunningham."

"So what do we know about Rachel Cunningham?"

"She divorced five years ago. Her ex, John, now lives in Australia. The breakup was probably triggered by a family tragedy. Their daughter, Kelly, was killed by a speeding car while walking to the school bus. Mrs Cunningham was one of the first at the scene. The child died before the ambulance could arrive."

"And the driver?"

"Fled the scene. Making it a hit and run on a cold and dark November morning with no witnesses. But he was caught when he put the vehicle into his local garage for repair. Tried, found guilty and sentenced to six months."

"Six months?"

"He had what his lawyer called personal problems. His mother had just died and he was distressed. Up to this point he'd been an exemplary citizen. The local council knew it was an accident black spot and had done nothing to reduce the risk to pedestrians. The school bus was parked in an inappropriate place. You get the idea."

"The judge bought it."

"In spades."

"We catch them and the ones with the money for clever lawyers walk free." Ives feels the need to move things on to hide his annoyance at this failure of the justice system. "What else do we have?"

"That's it so far, Steve. Just that Cunningham must have had something to hide, otherwise why the name change and why the pretence that she never had a child? I need more time to dig back into the case."

Ives nudges Lesley to let her know that the traffic ahead is beginning to move. "So, we talk to Mary Duggan."

They leave their vehicle in the University visitors' car park and make their way to Chemistry. Ives feels as out of place here as he does in the mortuary. Perhaps, after all, it's something about science rather than the smell of dead bodies that affects him so much.

Mary Duggan has done well. The sign on the door reads *Professor M. Duggan.*

She looks up from the student reports she's correcting as Ives and Lesley come in. "I've been told you're here about Isobel Cunningham?"

Ives leads the questioning with Lesley taking notes. "You and Mrs Cunningham studied together and remained close?"

Mary Duggan peers over her reading spectacles. "Not close, especially after she married. But we kept in touch. Since her divorce we've become closer again."

"The phone records show you're the one she calls most frequently."

She smiles. "Is that so? Perhaps she doesn't make that many calls."

"Any idea why she changed her name?"

"You mean when she married John?"

"No, when she started calling herself Isobel rather than Rachel."

"She always preferred Issy to Rach amongst her friends, all the way back to when we were at university. That's not a new kind of crime, is it?" She pauses. "But, Inspector, you still haven't told me why you're here. Is Issy in some kind of trouble?"

"She's had a shock. She's in King's College Hospital."

Duggan gives a nervous shudder, affected by the news. "I must go see her."

"No visitors until the doctor says so."

She gives a wry smile. "If I phone her, no doubt you'll be monitoring the call?"

Ives smiles back. "You know that's not the way this works. We'd need a special order from the Home Secretary."

"As the Home Secretary herself keeps trying to assure us. There aren't many left out here that believe that any more." She pauses. "So, what do you want from me?"

"Did Isobel Cunningham visit you here?"

"Why do you ask?"

"It's something we need to know."

"Well, the answer is, of course, yes. We sometimes met here before heading out for coffee."

"And how recent was that?"

She scratches her head. "Well, let me think. Early last week."

"And before that?"

"Maybe ten days."

Ives leans forward in his seat. "Do you have potassium chloride here?"

"Why do you ask me that?"

"Let's say it could be important to our investigations."

"Well, yes, of course. It's a common reagent. We use it as an electrolyte in all manner of applications. In solution, it's the filling agent in our pH and oxygen sensors, for example."

"And where is it kept?"

"In our chemical store, along with a hundred and one other reagents. This is a Chemistry department, Inspector."

"And if I went out into the labs amongst your researchers and students, what are the chances that I'd be able to find a bottle or two of potassium chloride alongside everything else?"

"Quite probable, Inspector. It's not a restricted substance. It's not flammable or poisonous. So no need to keep it locked away."

"So, Mrs Cunningham could have had access to it while she was visiting you here? Let's say, if she wanted to acquire some for any reason?"

"I suppose she could. But why would she want to do that?"

"Leave that to us, Professor Duggan."

As they return to the station, with Lesley once more having to find a route through the dense London traffic, Ives comes to the point. "In addition to the surveillance paranoia we've come to expect from academics, Duggan seemed defensive."

"She's protecting a friend. That's only natural."

"From what? We didn't tell her of any suspicions we might have."

Lesley smiles. "That's something that never ceases to amaze me about you, Steve. How don't you get it that when people are questioned by the police, suspicion is never far from their minds."

Ives takes a message from his phone. "Word from King's College. Mortimer says we can speak to Cunningham."

# CHAPTER 33

The nurse tells me the police are here to ask questions.

"It's nothing you should worry about. If you feel it's too much you just have to say stop and Mr Mortimer will tell them to leave."

I don't know what use I can be to them. They'll be concerned about my past. Isn't that what police always want to know? And what will I be able to tell them?

The ghosts of my past have pushed and pulled and played with my feelings of guilt. But they haven't stayed for long enough.

The most of what I know for sure is written in the notes I keep on the phone and I'm not about let the police know about that.

The tall one introduces himself as Detective Inspector Ives and he tells me that the woman with him is Detective Sergeant Lesley. They must have agreed to let Lesley take the lead since she starts asking the questions.

"Mrs Cunningham. Can I call you Issy?"

I nod. "I guess so. Most people do."

"You wouldn't prefer us to call you Rachel?"

"Why would you want to do that?"

"We know you've been through a traumatic experience. I want to assure you that we're aware of that and wouldn't be here unless it was absolutely necessary. There are some questions we need to ask about what happened to Mike Aspinal."

"He died."

"You're aware of that?"

I nod again. "That's why you're here."

"How do you know?"

"Know what?"

"That he died. Mr Mortimer says you have problems with your memory."

"Colin told me. Colin Tempest."

"You remember Mr Aspinal being killed?"

"No, I didn't say that. I said Colin told me that."

"You know how he died?"

"A heart attack."

"And how do you know that?"

"I can't recall. Colin must have told me."

"But you do recall going out with Aspinal the day before Valentine's Day."

"No."

"He took you to a bar in Soho."

"I'd never do such a thing."

The tall one, DI Ives, interrupts. "If you don't mind me saying, Issy, you did go out with him, didn't you? Why would you want to lie about a thing like that? You don't strike me as the kind of woman who would want to do that."

I don't like what he's implying. "What kind of woman might that be, Inspector? What gives you the right to be so judgmental?"

He backs off. He sounds apologetic but I don't believe him. "I'm sorry, I didn't want it to come out like that. Was there some reason why you don't want to tell us you were with him?"

I shake my head. "No. I told you, I don't remember."

DS Lesley gives Ives a look that says: *Leave this to me.* "You went to the bar in Soho. We can prove that. And after that?"

"How would I know?"

"You went back to the office."

"If you say."

"You remember him touching you?"

I lower my head. What she's saying is hitting home, hurting me deep, digging into what I can't forget. But I give a different answer. "No."

"We know he was the one who raped you, Issy. We know you were with him at Ardensis in the hours before he died. I'm here to tell you that if you need it we have people who can help."

"I don't know about any rape. I don't need help. I just want to be left alone."

"I'm afraid we have a few more questions before we can do that."

I appeal to Lesley, woman to woman. "Do you know what it's like to go through what I'm going through? Do you?"

Lesley tries to sound comforting. "Maybe we should continue tomorrow, or the day after, when you feel better about this?"

"You still don't get it, do you? I blame myself for what happened. Why I've ended up here."

"As I said, let's talk about this tomorrow."

Ives pulls out a photograph and shows it to me. "We found this in your apartment, Issy. This is you, with a child. We think the child must be your daughter, Kelly."

I look away and begin to cry. "Why are you doing this to me?"

There's a noise behind them as Mr Mortimer comes in. "That's enough, Inspector. My patient needs to rest. You'll have to complete your questioning later in the day."

Ives complains but the doctor demands that they leave and return no sooner than in three hours.

I watch as the two officers are shown away.

When I stop crying, I make a note on the phone.

*DI Ives behaves like he's planning to arrest me.*

# CHAPTER 34

There are no sounds in the corridor outside the room.

I've been sleeping again. I've lost track of how much time has passed since Ives was here asking questions. But from the rhythm of the hospital, it must be late in the day.

I stare at the last note on the phone.

*DI Ives is behaving like he's planning to arrest me.*

I know I can't stay.

I scroll through the messages and pause at the picture of Mary Duggan.

She's my friend. She'll know what to do.

I climb out of the bed and search for my things in the bedside cabinet. As I hoped, they are all here.

I dress and walk out of King's College. Though there are people all around – doctors, nurses, ancillaries and patients – all are occupied with their own reasons for being here and no one stops me.

As I step outside the hospital, the clamour of the London street burns my senses. I'm not expecting the raging disorder that surrounds me, forcing me back into the dark shell of my self.

I begin to panic, to tell myself that this is a mistake. I should stay and face Ives.

I take deep breaths and hail a passing black cab. When it pulls up at the kerb, I climb inside and ask for Charing Cross. It's the first name that comes into my head.

At first I'm sure that the driver is talking to me as he pulls the cab out into the traffic, but I realise that he's in animated conversation with someone on the other end of the Bluetooth pod that he wears in his ear. The fact that I'm now in the cab is of little consequence to him.

I sit back in the seat. I try to collect my thoughts.

Mary Duggan's Facebook page says she works at University of London, Department of Chemistry.

I bang on the sliding glass partition that divides the passenger space from the driver's side and, with reluctance, he interrupts his conversation to pull it back.

"I need to go somewhere different."

He snarls back. "You mean you don't want me to take you to Charing Cross?"

I tell him Mary's address and he makes a great show of swerving the taxi against the traffic and into an elaborate U-turn that heads us off in the opposite direction.

"University of London it is."

He can't wait to return to his Bluetooth conversation and, without saying anything more, he snaps the sliding partition shut.

I search through the bag. Not much here. Enough to pay the taxi but not enough to last out here for long.

I pull out the phone and call Mary Duggan.

She picks up.

"Mary, it's me, Issy."

"I was coming to see you."

"I'm out. We need to meet."

Mary sounds unfazed. "OK. Let's meet at the usual place."

I don't know what she means. "Tell me where that is."

"The Golden Eagle, the pub close to the university where we usually meet."

I try to pretend I knew this all along. "OK, see you there."

I bang on the sliding partition once more and, this time, I can see from the anger with which he pulls out the Bluetooth earpiece that the driver is not going to even try to be helpful.

"You've changed your mind again."

"I need to meet someone at the Golden Eagle."

"OK. You know the clock's running and this is going to cost you?"

When I reach the pub, it's crowded and there is no sign of Mary.

I tell myself that she needs time to get here. I try to recall where she lives, to work out how long she might take, but nothing comes.

I decide that all I can do is wait.

I push my way through the crowd at the bar and try to look like any other customer waiting for a drink. When my turn comes I ask for a martini. I get a sideways stare from the old man standing next to me that says: *We don't drink that here.*

The martini comes from a bottle. The only choice is ice or no ice. I go for ice.

I try to stop myself thinking that everyone here is looking at me and wondering: *what's someone like her doing here?* Or, worse: *Isn't she the one the police are coming to arrest?* I try to tell myself that this was what happens when you've been through whatever it is that makes me feel as I do – abandoned, hurt, alone.

As I move away from the bar and back through the crowd, I feel a hand on my shoulder.

I turn. It's Mary.

"Issy. What on earth have you got yourself involved in?"

"Mary. I don't know where to start. My whole world has fallen apart."

She leads me to a quiet room at the back of the pub where we find a table.

Mary stares at the martini that now rests between us on the tabletop. "I didn't know you liked that."

"I'm not sure I do. It was the first name that came into my head."

"It's as bad as that?"

I nod. "Things have happened that I can't recall. And what I do get to remember, I can't hold onto for long. It makes the world a frightening place. And, Mary, the worst thing is, it's all my fault."

Mary looks back, puzzled, as if she's trying but failing to understand. "So, you can't tell me what's wrong?"

I pull out the phone from my bag. "I only have this.

I show her the notes on the phone.

Her eyes widen as she reads.

*Why did Colin need my help?*
*Mary is a good friend.*
*I should have trusted my mother.*

*John, how did I ever lose you?*
*Mike is dead.*
*Why do I feel so guilty?*
*Colin behaves like he owes me.*
*How I love you, Kelly.*
*Kelly, can you ever forgive me?*
*I know I won't see John again.*
*Mike is dead.*
*Colin behaves like he owes me.*
*I know why I hate Mike.*
*Colin is holding back on me.*
*Mike raped me.*
*DI Ives is behaving like he's planning to arrest me.*

She looks back up. "This is what you know for sure?"

I shake my head. "This is *all* I know."

"You were raped?"

I nod and say nothing more.

She places her arms round me. "I'm so sorry, Issy. You're being very brave. Ives said nothing about that."

"He's been to see you?"

"Yes." Mary reads over the list again. "You've been through a terrifying time, Issy. So bad I can barely imagine. But there's one thing I already understand. You need to stop blaming yourself."

"But it is my fault. It's all my fault. If I'd stayed away from him, this wouldn't have happened. If I'd been a better person, I wouldn't be like this now."

She softens her voice. "I don't want you to take this the wrong way, Issy, as any kind of criticism. Tell me you're not just running away from the past like you have before."

"You're talking about Kelly?"

"I didn't want to take you there, Issy. But you have her name on the notes on your phone. You're not somehow trying to run away from those same old problems all over again?"

I'm now more confused and I feel even more like breaking down in tears. In this moment, Mary knows more about me than I do myself.

I struggle to find an answer. "You're right. I'm running away. I feel the pain of losing Kelly all over again whenever I hear her name. That loss is engrained in every day, every night. Nothing's going to change that. But I'm not running because of Kelly."

"Then why?"

"I'm running from myself. What I've done."

She puts her arm around me again. "Here's what you need to know. People who've been abused often blame themselves. Especially women. It's part of who they make us think we are. And it's part of the grieving and repair process.

I can feel her strength flowing into me. But I don't want to believe her. "Mary, I know you're trying to protect me. And I know I'm weak. What's happened leaves me unprepared to take on the world. My memory is shot. I see my past as splashes of light and colour on a dark, endlessly receding background." I pause to take a deep breath. "But you know, Mary, the one thing that's certain is that I'm not a killer and I'm not about to wait and let someone like DI Ives bend the truth to show that I am." I pause again. "I can tell that Ives is certain I killed Mike Aspinal."

"Aspinal?"

"The new boss. The stand in for Vince while he's away. The one who attacked me."

"Bastard deserved it if he's the one who raped you."

I point to the notes on the screen. "He did. He did."

Mary gives me a hug. "I'm sorry, Issy. Sorry to make you go through that."

"So, that's why I'm here. And I don't know where to turn next."

Mary sits up straight. "Don't worry. I can help. But you have to get real."

"What do you mean?"

"Tell me, how did you get here?"

"Took a taxi to Charing Cross. Then asked the driver to bring me here."

"Stop anywhere on the way?"

"No."

"OK. There will be camera footage as you left the hospital. The taxi you took will almost certainly have its own camera. And, of course you phoned me. You won't have long before the police get a fix on you."

I hold up my hand. "Stop, Mary. It's as bad as that?"

She leans forward in her chair. "Not if we move quickly. We can't be seen together after this. Ives will try to find you via me, that's if he doesn't track you down via surveillance."

"Then, I need to disappear. Maybe I should try a cheap hotel."

Mary shakes her head. "Too risky." She lowers her voice. "I know someone in the East End who might be able to help."

"You trust them?"

"I do. And you'll feel the same once you meet him. Promise."

"So, what now? You haven't had a drink."

"No time for that." She holds out her hand. "Give me your phone. It's too dangerous for you to use it again. And I have an idea how we can use it to slow Ives down."

I start to panic. "But I need the notes. It's all I can be sure of."

She pulls out a mini tablet from her pocket and copies the notes from the phone into an app there. When she's finished, she hands the tablet over. "There you are. All there, just as you made them."

I hand her the phone. "Thanks, Mary."

"Time to leave before Ives traces you here."

# CHAPTER 35

Justin Hardman dislikes admitting to himself that this is personal, but in the case of Vincent Blakemore it is.

He knows he's breaking every rule. Business should be about business and nothing else. The wealth his family is owed, everything that has been taken from them with such lack of concern for the inevitable effects upon them, has to be recouped. This is the article of faith that sustains him. The individual players involved are not important. It's the money that matters.

But, though he knows it's wrong, he's forced to make an exception for the Blakemores. Two generations back, in the Thirties, Henry Blakemore, Vincent's grandfather, pushed the Hardman legacy to the limit and beyond. The case for punitive damages in a failed business deal over the importation of cotton from Egypt bankrupted the Hardmans, coming as it did on top of the losses on Wall Street that reduced the business to a perilous state. The Hardman property seized, the Hardman assets stripped, the family left all but destitute. Justin Hardman's father raised a pauper. The reason why Hardman himself was born into a world that knew only hardship, struggle and despair.

Hardman looks at himself in the mirror. Who would guess what he's been through to get to where he is now? The people he's been forced to hurt. The lives he's had to dislocate. The cunning he's had to show to begin to regain his place.

So, yes, there is nothing accidental in the targeting of Ardensis, that so much cherished outcome of Vincent Blakemore's time in this world. His life's work.

The company founded on the wealth stolen from the Hardmans all those years before.

It was more than necessary to take Ardensis down. To pauperise Blakemore. It was Hardman's duty and destiny to do so.

And, yes again, he'd been thorough. He'd left no room for mistake. He'd used his power and influence to dig into the background of each and every one of the company employees. Bribing where necessary. Pressurising where necessary. Threatening where necessary. Assembling each and every last inconvenient truth about each and every one of them so that when the time came to act, he could be sure that the help he needed would not be refused.

And now the one thing he couldn't foresee. The Cunningham woman intervening just when he was in touching distance of righting a wrong that had persisted for too long.

Someone has to pay.

It has to be her.

# CHAPTER 36

DI Lesley ploughs the car on through the driving rain and is not pleased.

"Steve. It's late. Gone ten. What are we doing?"

"Going to arrest Issy Cunningham. Would have done it earlier if that interfering doctor hadn't stepped in."

"But I thought you'd accepted that we can't do that yet."

He takes a deep breath. "I've been picking away at that and can't let it rest. We have the motive. We have the murder weapon and we know that she had the opportunity to use it."

"But you can't explain why she had the syringe and the poison there, ready and waiting."

He tenses. "Look, June. No investigation is perfect. You know what they say: if everything fits it's a sure sign that there's something very wrong. We have enough. The rest will come out when we question her."

"She's a traumatized woman. You wouldn't want to put her through the mill, would you, Steve? How's that going to look when the Court gets to see the video of the interview?"

"OK. So we need to be careful. Sensitive, even. I'll let you ask the questions."

She smiles. "So what do you expect to find. Exactly."

"What do you mean, *exactly*. Sounds like you're still on her side."

"I'm not defending her, Steve, I'm just saying."

"And I'm saying once she confesses, she'll tell us how she did it."

"*If* she confesses."

"OK. If."

They arrive at the hospital. The visitor car park is full.

Lesley curses.

Ives smiles. "Leave it outside the front entrance, June. Who's going to book us?"

Inside they find Mortimer. He looks perplexed. "There's a problem, Inspector. Mrs Cunningham is nowhere to be found in the hospital."

Ives demands to see the room. He curses when he finds it empty. "Do we know when she left?"

Mortimer shakes his head. "The last record on her chart is at eight thirty. So, some time after that."

Ives can't let it go. "I thought your patients were under constant supervision."

"That's true. But we're short staffed. These things happen."

Ives and Lesley travel back to the Lions Yard station in silence.

Ives speaks first. "If she didn't do it, why did she decide to run?"

# CHAPTER 37

Mary Duggan parks in a side street off the Commercial Road, close to the Troxy dance hall.

From the back seat she produces the brown corduroy coat and hat that she tells me she keeps in her vehicle for emergencies and she hands them to me.

"Ives will have sent out a description of you by now. He'll know what you were wearing from the videos of your leaving the hospital and from the taxi ride. Wearing these will confuse him as best we can."

I push my hair up inside the cap, pat it down on top of my head and pull down the peak. I turn up the collar of the coat. "How do I look?"

Mary smiles. "Very Francois Hardy."

"You'll get cold with no coat."

Mary shakes her head. "No, this is as far as I go, Issy. This is where we part." She pauses. "There's no video surveillance here. So, even if at some point in the future Ives uses number plate recognition on this vehicle and tracks our trip here, he won't be able to discover your next pick up and where you go next."

She reaches into the glove compartment, pulls out a roll of notes and hands them to me.

"Take this, use it when you need to and don't go near an ATM."

I stare at the thick bundle of notes. "Where do these come from, Mary?"

She smiles. "It's always worth keeping cash. In case of emergencies. In case the banks run out. I thought everyone was doing that now."

"I could have withdrawn my own."

"That's exactly what Ives is expecting you to do. The whole system of ATMs is transparent to the police. Quickest way of giving away your location. And each and every one is fitted with its own networked video surveillance. So they also get to know if you've changed your appearance."

I accept the money. "I'll pay you back."

An old Ford truck draws up behind.

A tall, slender man jumps down from the driver's seat and hurries towards us.

I find myself whispering. "Who's this?"

Mary smiles. "This is the friend I told you about. His name's Adam. Adam West. He'll take care of you."

There's an inrush of cold air as the newcomer opens the rear door of Mary's vehicle and jumps in.

Adam says little. He gives an engaging enough smile as Mary introduces him but he is no more demonstrative than that.

Mary gives me a final embrace. "You're in safe hands now. Adam will take you to his place in Limehouse Basin. You can depend on him."

"Thanks, Mary. I don't know how I can ever repay you."

"Just get well. See this thing through."

Adam West is a careful driver. He takes considerable care pulling the Ford out onto the busy Commercial Road and makes a point of maintaining the recommended distance from vehicles in front once he joins the stream of traffic.

With Mary's help and no longer being confined in the hospital, I'm beginning to feel stronger, more able to relate to what is around me. I can hear Mr Mortimer's words. *Hold on. You will feel better.*

I feel confident enough to try to open up the conversation. "Adam, I want to thank you for helping me."

He holds his attention on the road ahead. "That's OK. Anything for a friend of Mary's."

"How do you know her?"

"She didn't tell you?"

"I don't think so."

"Well. I was a student of hers. At the University. Ten years ago. We've remained friends since."

Most of what I should know about Mary is still lost to me. I struggle to recall anything of substance about her. Then, I recall that that I've seen her address. "So, Chemistry?"

He nods and then falls silent.

"And so you're a chemist?"

"No. I'm more interested in computing."

"And that's what you do?"

"Yes."

I can see that he's uncomfortable answering questions about himself and that he has little need to ask questions of me.

I try again. "You haven't asked."

"Asked what?"

"Why I'm here, on the run like this."

He shakes his head. "Mary told me. I get the picture."

"What did she say?"

"That you're a good friend. That you're wanted by the police. And that I should find out all I can about Ardensis."

"That's all?"

He nods again. "That's enough."

"Won't the police be able to find you from the contact she made to ask you to help me?"

He smiles. "We use an encrypted message app. Sends the authorities wild. They're doing all they can to close it down, but it's still there and we use it. So, no need to worry."

He pulls the Ford into a side street, finds an alleyway leading from it and draws up in front of a line of lock-up garages. "We walk from here."

With the Ford stowed away in the lock-up, Adam shows me the short cut to Limehouse Basin. "No cameras along here."

I'm surprised by what I see next. Rising almost from nowhere, right here in the heart of the city, approached from a staircase of steps that leads off the busy road, is a marina filled with vessels of all shapes and sizes. Some are yachts that must command million pound price tags. Many are more humble vessels. Adam points to one of the narrowboats, the one with the name *Diamond Matrix* on the bow.

"There she is."

From the moment I step aboard, I feel secure. Perhaps it's something to do with the compactness of the vessel and the fact that this just feels like a place to hide.

"I have to tell you, Adam. I'm going to *like* it here."

He smiles. "It's still two hours 'til dawn. We could both do with sleep."

He points towards the couch at the centre of the vessel. "Turns into a bed. I can sleep here, if you like. You can take the bedroom at the stern."

I hold up my hands. "No, Adam, I'll be OK on the couch. Promise."

# DAY 3

# CHAPTER 38

I wake to the sound of breakfast being made.

I'm coming round from the deepest, dream-filled sleep. Perhaps it's the gentle swaying of the boat on the mild currents in the marina that helps to make the feeling of abandon so complete.

I sit up on the couch and know I've been doing more than dreaming. My past has been returning to me. At least, most of it.

It's strange. I can now look back on the last forty-eight hours and have my first real notion of how it has been. How it felt in that cold, dark emptiness where I'd been left without a past, without a future. I understand now that was something close to having no soul.

If I close my eyes I can see myself then. I can feel the stark terror of not knowing where I am or where I'm going. I can look back and see that other person. The person that I was.

And then, a second wave of revelations comes with a nagging bite of reality. There are things that sleep cannot change. I'm being sought by the police. Mike Aspinal has raped me. Inspector Ives is seeking to arrest me for Aspinal's murder.

I call out to Adam. "What time is it?"

"Almost eleven. You needed the sleep." His eyes move in the direction of the stern. "You can freshen up, if you like."

"That would be good."

He smiles. "I'll give you a guided tour. I don't think you took much of this place in last night."

Everything about the *Diamond Matrix* is a surprise. Adam is right. For all intents and purposes, I'm seeing it for the first time.

So much has been fitted into such a cocooned space. There is a compact but well-featured galley style kitchen at the centre of the long, narrow, fifty foot long interior. At the stern end of the narrowboat is a sleeping area with nearby toilet and shower and, at the bow end, a living area with the couch and a coffee table, a solid fuel-burning stove and, nearby, a desk that houses Adam's computer with shelving filled with books.

As Adam tells me, what's more remarkable is that, while the *Diamond Matrix* has been moored here in the Limehouse Basin Marina for more than a year, its engines are still in good working order and, at any time, he could cast off and head for the world beyond.

This is a place of secure hiding. But also a point of escape.

It's clear this is Adam's prize possession. "More people are taking on narrowboats, living on the water. You can still buy one for under fifty thou. That's a bargain compared with anything you can get within a twenty mile radius of here. And you're right in the heart of the East End, no more than fifteen minutes from Canary Wharf."

He leaves me to freshen up at the stern. The pain is still there in my abdomen. A constant reminder of what has been.

When I return, Adam serves breakfast of scrambled egg and toast with coffee. It's one of the best meals ever.

"That was wonderful, Adam."

He smiles in recognition.

I glance at the computer. "You're connected?"

"High speed broadband. The Basin Authority runs it from their office on the dock. Life on the water doesn't have to mean you're cut off from the world any more." He pauses. "And don't worry about security. I use encrypted proxy sites to mask where I go on the Internet. Any activity from here is just about as close to invisible as can be. And there's nothing to connect you to me. You're safe here."

"I do feel safe. What's more important is I feel like myself. What did Mary tell you about me?"

"As much as I need to know."

"Well, what's important is whatever she told you is changing. I can't say I've come to terms with what happened. Perhaps I never will. But I can begin to look back and make new memories just like anyone else. It's slow and painful but it's starting to happen, just as my doctor told me it would. And, when I look back, I realise now that in the dark place I was in, I could do neither of those things. That's what was so terrifying, that I could lose the right to do these things that everyone takes for granted."

I pull out the mini tablet that Mary gave me and show him the notes I've made. "Before today, this was all I knew for sure."

He looks over the list and shows no surprise at what he sees.

"I now know so much more. Every one of those events sets off a stream of associations."

"You're back as you were before all this happened?"

"Not yet. But I'm much closer than I was yesterday. Part of that is being here, feeling safe. Allowing myself to believe that trauma is not waiting just round the corner. But when I look, I know there are still gaps in what I can recall. I don't know if it's because there are things I don't want to see, or if the gaps will be there for longer than I would have hoped. I don't want to think about that too much right now. Nor do I want to bask for too long in the glow of how much better I feel today than yesterday. I want to find the truth about what happened to me."

He smiles. "I understand."

"And I know I can depend on you to help."

"Of course, as Mary told you." He pauses. "In fact, I've already started. While you were sleeping I was checking out Ardensis."

I can't avoid the thought that he's steering me with great care away from my most immediate worries. "What kind of checks?"

"Hacking into the servers there to take a first look at their email traffic and web usage."

I move closer to Adam's computer. "You can do that from here?"

He nods. "It's not that legal but it is very revealing. The recent traffic is dominated by Mike Aspinal's death, of course. Most is what you'd expect. Messages passing back and forth about the police being involved and the fact that they've concluded that he was murdered."

"Any more details?"

"Not much more than that."

"Much about me?"

"No more than you would expect. Sympathy at first, then surprise that you've gone missing."

"Word travels fast. Anything on what the police are now saying about me?"

He shrugs. "I haven't looked at that yet. I can try if you like."

"No. It can wait. Anything more on Ardensis?"

"There's a mass of business detail, much of it trivial, I guess, and the kind of material that would take weeks to process. But one set of messages stands out because it's encrypted."

"So we can't read them?"

"That's right. You need the encryption key, otherwise the message looks like just a jumble of code." He pauses. "But, everything doesn't get encrypted. The headers with the email address and subject line stay as they are"

"So you can see who they're talking to?"

He nods. "Not quite. You can see their email address but not their name. And most of those addresses are chosen not to lead to a name. I've been digging around all over the web, looking to see if I can find that connection. So far, I can only be sure of one of the names. Aspinal himself."

"And Aspinal exchanged how many of these messages?"

"Over a hundred and fifty. And they get more frequent, right up to the time of Aspinal's death."

"So, how many people was Aspinal exchanging encrypted messages with?"

"Up to a dozen whose email addresses we know but not their names. I'll make a printout of the headers. Let me know what you make of it. You may see a pattern in who he was talking to, or recognise them from the addresses."

# CHAPTER 39

Lesley takes little convincing that they should spend time interviewing Mr Mortimer again.

Ives is clear what he wants. "Cunningham is out there somewhere and we don't know where she is. Yesterday she was banged up in hospital, barely able to move under her own steam, yet alone evade the Met. So we need to know what's changed."

Lesley agrees. "OK, Steve. I get it. We're not medics. We need to speak to someone who is." She pauses as she pulls their car out of Lions Yard and into the line of traffic. "I called Mortimer and he's agreed to see us straight away provided we can get there before his ward round at ten."

"And that should be easy enough so long as we don't get snarled in this traffic."

"You don't fancy the siren?"

"We're not that desperate, June. And in any case, you know it won't make a lot of difference."

Mortimer is waiting for them in a side room at King's College.

Ives jumps straight in. "Tell me, Mr Mortimer, what would you expect Issy Cunningham's condition be right now, as we speak."

The young doctor gives an amiable smile. "Does that mean we're forgiven for losing her?"

"That was yesterday. This is today. She's still on the loose. I wouldn't have thought it possible she could have recovered as quickly."

"That's something we could have expected, Inspector. What we know about TGA tells us it's like that. The initial dislocation in the patient's life is so drastic that it's easy to assume they're going to stay that way for some time. They know who they are, all the personal details of their life, but that's all they know. They have no past and, what makes things worse, they find it impossible to make new memories. So they ask the same questions over and over and become distressed when people find that strange. But there's nothing permanent about this state of affairs."

"So, now she's recovered her memories, is that it, like flicking a switch?"

"Not quite. But that's not too far off. The recovery can be rapid and be almost complete. And it normally takes place within twenty four to forty eight hours of the initial attack."

"You say almost?"

"In the patients we've studied, the recovery can vary widely. From complete recall on this short forty-eight hour time scale to a partial recall that then gradually fills itself out over a matter of months. There doesn't seem to be any pattern that determines which type to expect."

"So Cunningham might have recalled everything that happened by now?"

"Indeed. Or, more likely, she has most of it but hasn't yet faced up to the most traumatic events. That's the most common response."

As they leave, Ives turns to Lesley.

Before he can speak, she interrupts him. "I know. There's no way we're going to know if she's lying to us if she says she doesn't recall what happened."

He nods. "That's right. But first we have to find her."

# CHAPTER 40

Marianne French regrets the day she met Malcolm Riches. Of course, she was flattered when he pulled her off the street and told her she was the most beautiful, most photogenic, girl he'd ever seen on the King's Road.

She was more than flattered when he offered her a career in modelling. That's the way she came to present it to herself. In truth, it didn't take long for Riches to let her know that he was more into glamour. What today you'd call soft porn. The world had changed. The old prudishness was a thing of the past. Why not show off her beautiful body? Artists like him needed that kind of freedom to express themselves. That's the way he'd spun it. Looking back, she had to admit that she swallowed his story whole. Especially when Riches convinced her that the quality of the work he produced would be so much the better if he had a personal knowledge of his subject. Which meant she should sleep with him. In fact, he swept her away and for a few weeks she was happy like never before. Posing for Riches by day and enjoying sex with him at night. Dreaming of the day when one of his photos of her would be recognized as the high art that it was and launching her career as a fashion model.

Looking back now, Marianne is ashamed at what she did. The photographs were tasteful of their type but showed more of her than she ever intended. Riches was taking photos of her she knew nothing about. There were images of her that left nothing to the imagination, no part of her anatomy unexplored. The first she knew of it, these started appearing in the top shelf magazines. Worse, Riches was videoing their lovemaking with hidden cameras and selling the results to pornographic web sites.

By this time, Riches was long gone, trawling the King's road for fresh talent.

That was twenty years ago. Marianne had done her best to change her appearance, wearing her hair short and dying it red. But the possibility of discovery still hangs over her as a dark shadow. What she fears most is that by some means her mother and father might get to see those photos or, worse, the videos.

The years have passed slowly. The material lost its currency as the succession of new girls appeared on the scene. Her hope was that the images of her passed into obscurity.

She established herself at Ardensis. She became more certain that her stupidity in being conned by Malcolm Riches was not going to result in any harm to her family or her career.

Then the phone call came.

Somehow Justin Hardman discovered the truth about her past. He had copies of the photos and the videos. He sent some 'samples' to her computer. The material looked dated now, as she expected, but it was still much too revealing. And there was no doubt that the one in the pictures was her, despite her being so much older now.

He didn't say what he wanted at first. When the time came for him to ask, she would have to do what he said or face the shame of her family and friends knowing how foolish she'd been.

It wasn't long before he told her what he wanted.

# CHAPTER 41

Adam gives me good news. "I've heard from Mary."

I look up from reading the printouts of the encrypted emails sent and received by Mike Aspinal that Adam has made for me. "You're sure that's safe?"

"As safe as safe can be."

"What does she say?"

"Your phone's on its way to Glasgow. Up and running. If the police are tracking it, as we're sure they will be, they'll think you've gone there. Which means the heat will be off for a few days here in London. You should be able to move around more freely."

"Thanks Adam. That's what I needed to hear."

I call him over and he sits beside me on the couch.

I've spent the past hour poring over the messages that passed between Mike Aspinal the others in the days before his death. The more I've seen, the more I've become confused at what I've found.

I show Adam the printouts. "I can't make much sense of them. It's like we're seeing less than one per cent of the story. I don't recognise any of the other email addresses. And why the encryption? Just what were they having to be so furtive about?"

"That's what we need to discover. We know when the encrypted messages started." He pauses to point to the relevant page. "There's nothing before January 8th. After that there's plenty."

I know what this means. "That's just a few days after Aspinal became CEO of Ardensis."

"Meaning that's when he had control of the company for the first time?"

"Yes. Vince, Vincent Blakemore, had left for the States. Aspinal was in control."

"And judging from the way the number of emails being sent is on a rising curve, I'd say that whatever they were planning was on the point of coming to a head round about now."

"But we're still no nearer to knowing what that was?"

"We aren't. But why not look at the core business? Ardensis is into advertising, right?"

I nod in agreement.

"So, let's make a wild guess and say this is about money. Most things in business are. Maybe they're plotting to steal advertiser accounts?"

I look back at Adam. My thoughts are drawn to what Colin Tempest was accused of by Mike Aspinal. I tell Adam. "There may have been problems with accounts leaving the company. Someone I know there, Colin Tempest, might have been involved. So, yes, that could be it. But why would something like that need such secrecy? And why are so many people involved?"

"I agree. It's not an easy fit." He leans back and stretches out his arms. "So, let's talk to Tempest. Hear what he has to say."

# CHAPTER 42

Ives takes a long gulp of coffee. "Any information on Cunningham's whereabouts?"

Lesley looks up. "Looks like a positive, Steve. We assumed she must have gone to ground somewhere in London but were surprised we weren't able to find her. Which makes this interesting."

She shows Ives the trace being made on the map that's displaying on her screen. "We're tracking her phone. And here it is, heading north out of London."

Ives gives a smile of satisfaction. "They never learn, do they? So, is she in a car, or on a train?"

"We don't know that yet, Steve. From the speed of movement, it could be either."

"OK. We'll track it 'til it stops and when it does, wherever she's running to, we'll alert the local force there and get them to pull her in." He pauses to wipe the back of his hand across his mouth. "In the meantime, where do we stand with the analysis of the syringe taken from Cunningham's desk?"

"That's just come through." Lesley looks down at her notes. "The report says that though the syringe was empty, there was residue of potassium chloride present, consistent with the notion that it had been filled with the liquid in the past." She pauses to sip some coffee herself. "And, here's the important part, the tip of the syringe is covered with Aspinal's DNA."

"And the solution?"

"The liquid used is indeed potassium chloride."

"Which means we have the murder weapon and the source of the chemical that killed him."

"Yes. But here's the thing, Steve. There are no fingerprints on the syringe."

"So, she wore gloves."

"Freudian slip. Steve?"

"OK. Whoever used it wore gloves"

"No gloves were found."

"Then get someone over there to find them. Or she could have thrown them away."

"So, why not throw away the syringe?"

"She was distressed. Traumatised. Becoming forgetful. She disposed of the gloves but forgot about the syringe."

Lesley gives Ives one of her looks that tells him there is more to come. "We still haven't come up with a good reason why she had all this stuff available to her in the desk drawer?"

"You're back to that again?"

"Why not. The basic issue hasn't changed. If we charge her with killing Aspinal, that's just what her defence counsel is going to say. They'll say that if she did it, she must have done that without leaving the building. Otherwise we'd have picked her up on the security camera footage from the lobby. So, the murder weapon, the potassium chloride and the syringe, must have been in her desk all along. And we won't have given the jury a good reason why she had it there."

Ives can see where this is going. "But they won't be able to prove that she didn't do it, given all the evidence we have that points to her."

Lesley smiles. "But that's not their job. It's up to us to produce a clear motive to explain why she did it."

Ives shuffles in the chair. "OK, she had some other reason to kill him. She must have been considering it anyway. Planning it, but not necessarily intending to go through with it. Once he rapes her, she makes up her mind."

"Then, it's not about rape. That's not the prime cause of what she did. If she did it. It's about something else."

Ives learns all over again the reason why he values these one-to-one sessions with Lesley so much.

"So, we need to discover what her real motive is."

"If she did it."

"You know she did it, June. Face facts, Stop trying to get her out of this."

"Just making a few points, Steve. That's all there is to it."

# CHAPTER 43

"I hope your mother is still well. No recurrence of her heart problems?"

These are the first words Marianne French is forced to hear as she joins Justin Hardman's table at the Blue Oyster.

He's playing with her. "Can't think what it might do to her. Seeing her daughter doing things an older woman might never have thought went on."

Frank Taylor, sitting beside Hardman, gives a tooth-filled grin. "Some things I never imagined went on. And I've not led a sheltered life."

Marianne curses again that she'd ever allowed those photographs of her to be taken and to be so naïve as to not suspect that Malcolm Riches was secretly filming their lovemaking. But what is done is done and she knows she has to live with it.

"What do you need, Mr Hardman? What can I do that I've not already been doing?"

He smiles. "It's true you've been a good girl. Keeping me informed about what's been going on at Ardensis. But you see, Marianne, things haven't worked out as they should. Aspinal is dead. And that means the deal can't go through. We didn't see that coming, did we? You could have warned me. You didn't do that, did you? And that's why we need this little talk. To see how we need to settle our account."

Marianne tries to not show her fear. "What more could I have done? No one saw this coming."

"You were working close to him. That's why you were of use to us. You must have noticed something was wrong."

"Everyone hated him. For what he'd become in such a short time since he was given power. How do you keep tracks on a man who has so many enemies?"

"That was your job. To let us know if anything was happening that was out of the ordinary. You let us down."

"Everything was out of the ordinary once Vince left for the States and Aspinal was in charge. Everyone was resentful at the way he used people, how he made all our lives a misery with his beloved rules. And the way he broke all those rules himself when it suited him."

Frank Taylor butts in again. "You didn't think it worth mentioning that Aspinal was involved with the Cunningham woman?"

Hardman intervenes before Marianne can reply. "You might not know this, Marianne, but I asked Frank here to follow Aspinal whenever he left the office. He saw Aspinal and Cunningham together in Soho on Valentine's Eve. Yet you told us nothing about that."

Marianne shivers. "I didn't think it mattered. It was just Aspinal doing what he thought he could get away with. Using his position to please himself."

Hardman doesn't look convinced. "And that's not anything to do with the fact that Cunningham is your friend?" Hardman's pupils focus down to pinpoints. "You see, we're hearing from our contacts in the Met that Cunningham is the one who killed Aspinal. If you'd told us what was happening we could have done something." He bangs his clenched fist on the table. "And then we wouldn't have lost the deal."

Marianne has no idea what the deal is. She just knows how important it is to Hardman and the certainty that he would make a lot of money if it went through. "What do you want me to do?"

"Someone has to pay. There's no way anyone leaves Justin Hardman out of pocket to the tune of a million and doesn't pay. You understand?"

Marianne repeats the question. "Just tell me what you want me to do?"

"If you don't want your mother to receive a package through her letter box showing her what a dirty slut her daughter has become, you'd better find out where Cunningham is. And do that while I'm still prepared to give you another chance."

# CHAPTER 44

It's raining as we climb down from the *Diamond Matrix* onto the jetty.

Adam raises a large multi-coloured umbrella for us both to shelter under. "Good for keeping out of sight of any security cameras that we might not know about."

We arrive at the lock-up still dry. I wait outside as he goes inside, starts up the Ford and drives it out onto the yard outside.

As I climb aboard, he's already programming the satnav. "Okay. We have Tempest's postcode. This boy will show us the way there."

The Tempest house is out in Ruislip, a thirty-minute journey according to the satnav. Adam winces. "Accurate to within a few metres in terms of location but hopeless in terms of the real world of travel traffic delays. I'd give it an hour."

As we work our way through the central London traffic heading for the M4 motorway, Adam is silent, concentrating on the difficulty of driving in London where each day the endless battle between cars, delivery vans, buses and cyclists reaches new heights of danger and distress for all concerned.

As we reach the motorway, he relaxes. "So tell me again, Issy, what's so special about Colin Tempest?"

"He's an important part of what happened. I know that. But I don't know the how and why. Does that make sense?"

"If it makes sense to you, that's good enough for me."

"When if I was in the hospital, I was in no state to understand what he was saying. He was asking me to make sure I covered something up. Something important to him. I need to know what that is."

We find the Tempest house in Cornwall Road, a quiet suburban street. It's a nineteen thirties semi as unremarkable as its neighbours with its neat garden and uniform décor. Not standing out is what matters here.

Adam drives past and parks a dozen houses down. It's still raining. We walk back to the Tempest house, again under the cover of the umbrella.

Adam rings the bell. There is no reply. He climbs over the gate at the side of the house and disappears from sight. He climbs back over a few minutes later. "No one home."

I'm disappointed. "So, what now?"

"We wait."

Adam knows about more than just computers. He knows how to defeat locks. He pulls out a multi tool from his breast pocket and begins to pick at the lock. "Unless people fit top of the range, there's not much to stop anyone with a little savvy from getting inside."

"What about the burglar alarm?"

He smiles. "I fixed that when I was round the back."

In a few minutes we're in.

"What now?"

Adam shows me to the front room. "Take a seat. Wait 'til he comes back. If he's been working at Ardensis as normal, he should be back within the hour." He pauses. "I'll be outside in the car." He hands me a phone. "Press hash to call me if you need to."

I sit back in the seat and listen to the silence of Colin's home. There is something uneasy about that silence. It gets louder the longer I wait.

I turn on the TV in the hope that there might be news about the events at Ardensis, but there is none. Mike Aspinal's death is routine enough to not merit a mention.

I soon tire of the news that tells me of the trouble that has overtaken the world in the past twenty-four hours. I have enough problems of my own.

I turn off the set and wait.

# CHAPTER 45

Stephen Ives can tell from the look on Lesley's face as she comes into his office that she has something important to tell him.

"Steve, I've been searching out more details on our murder victim. And I have something you need to see."

She places two photographs side by side on the table.

Ives turns them round so he can take a close look at each. "Two photos of Mike Aspinal. He looks younger in one and his hair colour is different. Auburn rather than black. But that's no crime."

Lesley smiles. "Except the younger, auburn-haired one went by the name of Mark Dankworth." She pauses for a moment. "I always thought there was something wrong about that Aspinal name. Didn't seem to fit the look of the man, if you know what I mean?"

"And you ran a facial recognition check and the software came back with this?" He waits for the pay off. "Changing your name is not illegal unless you're doing it deliberately to deceive, so what else have you found?"

"Just that Mark Dankworth was charged with dangerous driving five years ago. Killed a young girl. Fled the scene. Had a good lawyer and a weak-minded judge."

Ives interrupts. "No such thing as a good lawyer, you should know that by now, June."

"OK. He had a *sharp* lawyer and a weak-minded judge. Got off with six months."

Ives can see where this is leading. "And the name of the victim of the hit and run?"

"Kelly Cunningham. Isobel Cunningham's daughter."

Ives gives a broad smile. "You know what this means, June? You've just compromised Cunningham's last hope, the very thing that you've been using to defend her."

"I'm not defending her, Steve."

"No matter. Cunningham will have known about him."

"I checked. She was traumatized by the death of her child, as you'd expect, and stayed away from the hearing when Aspinal, or should we call him Dankworth, came to court."

Ives isn't going to be deterred. "But when the verdict was announced, there's no way she wouldn't have clocked the man, taken at least one long look at a face she was never going to forget. The certainty is it took time, but somehow she found him at Ardensis, took a job there herself, watched him, waited. Got ready to kill him for what he did."

"You don't know that. And for any of that to happen, Aspinal must have been unaware it was her, the mother of the child he killed."

"Come on, June. Don't tell me you haven't also checked into how likely that is?"

"You know me too well not to think that's not the next thing I'd do, Steve. So, yes, I did check. Cunningham was too distressed to attend the hearing, as we already know. Aspinal's lawyers were skilled at keeping the story out of the press. The case was only reported in the local papers. Images of Aspinal but none of Cunningham. So, it's a fair bet that Aspinal wouldn't recognize her when she took the job at Ardensis."

"And being the arrogant bastard that we've found him to be, he was the type who would have believed he could shrug the whole thing off as if it had never happened. Forget about the whole thing as quickly as he could." Ives pauses. "One thought, though. He didn't recognize her by name?"

Lesley shakes her head. "Guess that's the reason why Rachel Cunningham became Isobel Cunningham."

"Which gives us her real motive for killing Aspinal."

"You can't be certain of that."

"Come on June, it's as close as you can get to a racing certainty. Why else would she be there, working at the same company? You can't call that coincidence?"

"No, Steve. I'm just presenting the evidence."

Lesley takes both photographs. "OK, Steve. I'll file these and check out Cunningham's Internet usage in the past year. Maybe we'll find more evidence there."

He leans back in his chair. "So, where is Cunningham now?"

Lesley checks her screen. "Still heading north."

"Keep tracking it, June. Once she stops we'll put out the call to bring her in."

Ives stands and begins to walk away but Lesley motions him to come back.

"Something else, Steve. I've been checking again on the camera surveillance footage in and around Ardensis."

"I thought we were done with that."

"I don't mean the footage from the entrance area. I mean footage from the streets surrounding the building."

"Why do that? Isn't life too short?"

"Maybe I do need to get a life, Steve. But accept it for what it is. This is what turns me on. Call it a search for completeness."

Ives can tell she's onto something more and sits down beside her. He takes in what she's looking at on the screen. The frozen image of a well-dressed man walking along the street outside the Ardensis building. "So, who is this?"

Lesley has that *told you you'd find this of interest* look on her face. "That, Steve, is Vincent Blakemore."

"OK, he's the CEO. Doesn't he have a perfect right to be there?"

"Normally, yes. But look at the date."

"You're viewing footage from February 12th."

"When, according to Marianne French, Vincent Blakemore was supposed to be out of the country."

"So what was he doing there?"

"That's something we need to ask him."

# CHAPTER 46

I sit up straight as I hear the key in the lock.

It's Colin coming in and moving about in the hallway and then in the kitchen. I want to surprise him. I remain where I am. I know that within a few minutes he'll make his way into the sitting room.

The door handle turns and he enters. His look is more one of shock than one of surprise. "Issy. What are you doing here?"

I make him wait before I reply. "We need to talk."

"How did you get in?"

"That doesn't matter."

He comes closer and sits opposite me. "Issy, are you alright?"

"I'm getting by. I need to ask you about what happened."

He begins to move even closer but I hold up a hand to keep him away.

He looks offended. "I'm only trying to greet you as any friend would."

"I don't want friendship, Colin. I want answers."

He's playing dumb. "To what?"

"To what you were thinking of when you asked me to go and see Mike Aspinal."

"Like I told you. He was going to sack me."

"What if you deserved it?"

He looks downcast, like a little boy caught doing something wrong. "I thought you were on my side."

"Maybe I still am. That's what I need to know."

He says nothing more, waiting for my next question.

I look him in the eye. "Why were you so concerned to keep what happened secret?"

He looks down at his hands. "Because I'm ashamed of what I asked you to do."

"Then, why did you ask me?"

"Because I had no choice."

"Like your family would suffer if you lost your job? Colin I've been here an hour. Had time to look around. There's no sign of them."

He looks like he's about to burst into tears. "Angie, my wife and our daughter Clara. There's a good reason why they're not here."

He tries to move closer once more. For the first time I feel afraid of what he might do. I hold up the phone Adam has given me. "Keep your distance, Colin. I have someone outside and on the other end of the line. I press hash, he calls the police. You understand?"

He backs off and holds up his hands. "No need to involve the police, Issy. I can explain."

"You deceived me. It's more than shame that means you need to keep this from the police, isn't it?"

He looks away. "OK. I owe you a proper explanation."

"It had better be good, Colin. You know what Aspinal did to me, don't you?"

"I didn't know he'd react like that. How could I? I knew he was bad. Power crazy. But I had no idea he'd go that far.

"That's what's left me where I am. Having to come to terms with the whole of my life being turned upside down." I take a deep breath. "Let's start from the beginning, Colin."

"I guess I'm in denial. Unable to face up to everything that's been happening."

"I don't believe you, Colin. Try again. Something better. Something closer to the truth."

He stares at me, long and hard. As if he were seeing me for the first time. "Believe me, you don't want to get involved in this any more deeply than you need to, Issy."

"Don't humour me, Colin. I'm already involved. You made sure of that."

His words come all in a rush once he's decided to open up to me.

"OK. I stumbled onto something. I didn't know how important it was, at first. Then I made a mistake. I took what I knew to Aspinal.

I knew he was involved in some way. I tried to put the burn on him. I needed money. I'm in debt, most of it spent on treatments for Angie's eyes. Debt collectors were trying to repossess this house. Still are. The money would keep the family together, keep our home. But Aspinal called my bluff. He told me I didn't know enough to cause him any real trouble and that I should never have dared to try to put pressure on him."

"Slow down, Colin. What had you stumbled upon?"

"It was when I was working on the Forerunner account. I picked up the phone one day, and there it was. Somehow the call had been patched through to my line. It was someone talking to someone in Accounts. I think it must have been Angela Westbury. Telling her what to do. Telling her to play her part in some kind of conspiracy. I couldn't tell what it was. But you know when something is wrong. Then she called him by name. She was saying something like, *Mr Hardman I've been doing all you asked. What more can I do?* It didn't take me long to find out who she was talking to. Justin Hardman. And that's why I didn't want to tell you about any of this, Issy. He's someone you don't want to get involved with. I wanted to protect you from him."

"This is what you took to Mike Aspinal, hoping he'd play ball with you?"

"It was foolish. I know that now. But I was desperate and I thought he'd pay me to keep quiet. I didn't expect him to go so far as to sack me."

"So what were Angela and Hardman talking about?"

"All I could tell is that whatever it was, Mike Aspinal was part of it."

"Something illegal? Something involving Ardensis?"

"Yes. But that's all I knew."

I realise that either he's good at telling a story or he's the wronged man I always thought him to be.

"And Angie and Clara, where are they now?"

He doesn't give me an answer. "I needed the job at Ardensis to have any chance of paying off my debts, keeping this house, keeping my family together. So I came to you. I thought you could make Mike Aspinal see sense. I'm sorry, Issy, so deeply sorry for what happened."

"Why the need to call me and ask me to keep quiet? It's more than shame, isn't it Colin?"

"Aspinal must have told Hardman that I was a problem. Hardman threatened me. Told me not to talk to the police. Threatened Angie and our daughter. They're safe for now at her mother's in Lichfield. But I live in fear and dread of Hardman discovering where they are."

He reaches out to hold my hand and I don't pull away. "Take care, Issy. Now that I've told you. Take care."

# CHAPTER 47

Ives is surprised to hear that Vincent Blakemore is here at Lions Yard to see him.

Blakemore is the type to try to take control of the meeting from the start. "Marianne French told me you were keen to talk to me, so here I am."

Ives offers him a seat facing his desk. "Just filling in background, Mr Blakemore. We've spoken to almost everyone at Ardensis except you. So, you might say we're trying to complete the picture surrounding Mike Aspinal's death."

"I'll be pleased to assist in any way I can, Inspector. But, as I think you know, I've been away, visiting family in the States, so I may not be of much help."

Ives shuffles in his seat. "Tell me, why you left Aspinal in charge while you were away. He didn't make a very good job of it."

"I couldn't have known that. He was my right hand man. Next in line. It was only logical to hand over the running of the company to him while I was away."

"While you recuperated?"

"I wouldn't put it that way. It was just a good time to take a break. I hadn't done that for the best part of twenty years."

"So, how did it work? Did Aspinal send you regular reports?"

"Yes, we held a weekly conference call. He provided details of all the business we'd done that week."

"And you trusted what he told you?"

"Why wouldn't I, Inspector?"

"And the business remained successful?"

"Indeed. In fact it's been going from strength to strength. Mike was good at his job."

"And you didn't get to hear that it was his bad treatment of the staff that was making this possible?"

"Aspinal stuck mainly to business. How our accounts were faring. How many new accounts we'd attracted. He wasn't much concerned with personalities. Just the numbers."

"So, you didn't get to hear about any conflicts in the company? Any threats that might have been made to Aspinal personally?"

"No, Inspector. We talked business, as I told you."

Ives pauses and makes a point of consulting the notepad before him. "Tell me, Mr Blakemore, when did you return to Ardensis?"

"This is my first day back in."

Ives searches the face of his man as he speaks, looking for any tell tale sign. "Then, why do we have camera surveillance footage from February 12th showing you in the street outside the Ardensis building?"

Blakemore smiles. "Oh, that, Inspector, is something I have to confess to. I misled Marianne and everyone at Ardensis about that. You see, I needed some time to go visit my father. He's in a care home in Maidenhead and I needed time with him. He's frail and might not be with us long. I knew that once I set foot back in the company there would be so much that needed catching up on that I'd never get away. So I pretended I was still in the States and went to see my father."

"That doesn't explain why you came close to the Ardensis building."

"It was a late decision, I must admit. I was about to go back in. Resume my responsibilities. But the closer I came to the building, the more I realised that my father needed me and that once I stepped inside, that was going to be impossible. So, I changed my mind, turned heel and headed for Maidenhead. I'm glad I did."

"We can check, Mr Blakemore. That you, in fact, visited your father."

"By all means, Inspector. By all means."

# CHAPTER 48

As we travel back into London, I tell Adam what I've learned from Colin.

Adam is sceptical. "And you believe him?"

"I don't want to. But I have to say, yes, I think I do. He's no great actor. I think he's genuine in what he's telling me."

"You trust what he said after what he did to you?"

Why does it always come back to this short but fragile word? Trust. These five letters that rule my life. "Yes, Adam. I trust what he told me despite what happened to me. He couldn't have known."

We fall silent for a while. The rain has stopped and it's getting dark. The oncoming lights of the vehicles in the opposite lane of the motorway pierce the gloom in discordant flashes that shine in my eyes.

I'm trying to fight it. To place my thoughts somewhere, anywhere else but I can't prevent the image of Kelly from overtaking my mind.

*My dear Kelly, lying damaged and dying in my arms.*

*Here's John, in tears, telling me he can't go on now that she's gone.*

*Now Aspinal, his lecherous face, his piercing eyes portraying nothing but lust as he calls me a stupid bitch and pushes me further down onto his office couch.*

*I'm hurting and in pain. He's gorged himself on the violence he's shown me. Become the beast that had been in hiding within him. Wrecked my life for a second time.*

*He deserves to die.*

*I'm crying. Collapsed on the chair at the desk in my workspace.*

*Somewhere, back in his office, Aspinal must be congratulating himself on his night's work.*

*Yes, he deserves to die. Yet I feel so weak. Do I have the strength?*

*I'm opening the desk drawer. Reaching into it for something.*

*Something I'm not ready to see.*

I know I have to hang on. I have to prevent these visions from overwhelming me.

I turn to Adam and concentrate on what's been troubling me since the meeting with Colin. "Tempest talked about Justin Hardman."

Adam looks away from the road ahead and stares at me for far longer than is safe. "Did you say Hardman?"

I nod. "He threatened Colin."

His eyes return to the road ahead. "That's the last thing I wanted to hear. You need to know that whatever troubles you have will have just got a whole lot worse if Justin Hardman is in any way involved."

"What do you mean?"

"He's a fixer of things that aren't broken. He's one of the most powerful operators on Canary Wharf. They say that moneymaking is less a science and more an art and, more times than most people would like to believe, it becomes a black art. That's where Hardman comes in."

"He's corrupt?"

"You might say that. They say his business is strong-arming people into going through with deals they've promised to complete on or honouring loans they were unwise to have agreed to in the first place."

"Using force?"

"Not Hardman himself. He's much too smooth and tricky a character for that. His currency is persuasion. He has others, like his main man Frank Taylor, to do the dirty work."

"Not someone you'd want as an enemy."

I tell Adam what I learned about Hardman from Colin. "Colin overheard him planning some kind of deal."

"And you know what that means?" He answers his own question. "Those encrypted emails are between Aspinal and Hardman."

We've left the motorway now and we're held up at traffic lights at the start of the Commercial Road.

Now the rain has stopped there will be no excuse to use the umbrella. I reach back onto the back seat of the car and pick up the hat and coat that Mary gave me.

It's the best protection for the walk back to the *Diamond Matrix*.

Back at the narrowboat, Adam busies himself making dinner in the galley while I look over the printouts of the encrypted emails once more.

I still can't make that much sense of them but I think I can begin to see a pattern now that we know the names of two of the players.

Adam comes in from the galley, remembering something. "Oh, I almost forgot, I can show you photos of Hardman and Taylor."

He goes over to the computer and selects the page he wants to show me. "This is Justin Hardman."

I look at the suave, almost effete face. "I can see the con man in him. Wouldn't trust him if he was the last man alive."

"And here's Frank Taylor."

I stare at the craggy face. A man to be feared. But, and I can't shake the thought, this is a face I've seen before.

I close my eyes.

*I'm back in the champagne bar in Soho with Mike Aspinal on Valentine's Day eve. And there he is. The man I now know as Frank Taylor. Sitting on a stool at the bar, looking over at us now and then, trying to make it seem like he isn't interested in us.*

I refocus on Adam. "Taylor worries me the most."

He doesn't ask me why. "Hardman is the one to be careful of."

Dinner is as good as breakfast. As with everything else he does, Adam is an accomplished cook.

When we've finished and have done the dishes, he pauses to rub his eyes. "It's getting late. I can take the couch."

I shake my head. "It's OK, Adam. I'll sleep just fine on it."

# DAY 4

# CHAPTER 49

I wake and look out through window of the narrowboat. It's a perfect, sunny day with dazzling shards of light playing across the wavelets whipped up by a keen breeze blowing through the harbour.

Adam is in the galley making breakfast. I think about going down there to help but realise that with the space available I'll be in the way.

I pause and wonder what to make of Adam West. The *Diamond Matrix* is a perfect place of escape but it lacks most signs of home. Everything is neat, tidy and in order. There are no personal photographs, no signs of any significant connections.

He comes in with two plates of scrambled egg, toast and coffee and sets them down on the table. "Same as yesterday, I'm afraid."

I sit beside him on the bench that faces the small table. "And just as delicious. You really are a remarkable person."

He looks away and doesn't reply.

I press on. "I know you don't want to say much about yourself, and I respect that. I don't want you to take this the wrong way, but I'm curious about you."

"Whatever."

"Why this, Adam? Why here? Living on a boat in the centre of London. Why not a more regular existence?"

"I told you. I *like* it here. I thought you did, too." He pauses and stops eating. "There are no complications. There's the boat and there's me and that's it. I have all I need."

"But most people need more."

"I have friends. People like Mary. People I know. No one close. You have a problem with that?"

"It's none of my business, Adam. I shouldn't be prying. I'm just curious to understand."

"Then, why so many questions? Why can't people take things for what they are? I promised Mary I'd help you. And, as anyone can see, you need help, you really do."

I realise I've gone too far. "I'm sorry, Adam. Sorry for asking so many questions." I take a deep breath. "You see, I've been let down by people I've given my trust to. I sometimes think that's some kind of punishment for what happened when people asked for my trust and I wasn't able to return it. If you can make any kind of sense of that."

"I'm trying."

"I think that's what makes me want to know more than I should about people."

"Like whether you can depend on them?"

"No, whether I'm in danger of betraying their trust."

He pulls his hand away as I try to hold it. "I know that people spend too much time pretending they understand each other when they really don't."

My attention is captured by one of the books in the case alongside us. There, next to paperbacks on Fortran C programming and biographies of Turing and Hawking, is a slender volume, *Living With Autism*.

I reach across and take the book down from the shelf.

"Do you mind?"

He agrees. "If you must."

"This is you?"

He nods. "I guess it is. If you need to know. I'm undiagnosed and prefer it that way. I've been lucky to escape the categorization that would have made me into some kind of case for treatment. I love my life and live it the way I want, the way I need to. That might not be the same way you'd choose to live yours. But it's my way. Right here, on this boat. Alone in your eyes. At peace in my own. And if I say I'm here to help, if I promise that to Mary, that's just what I'm here to do. And, yes, you can trust me."

I want to hold him, to say I'm sorry for doubting him, but I realise that's not a possibility.

I decide to change the subject. "So, where do we stand after what we learned from Colin Tempest?"

Adam starts to look more comfortable. "Well, he told you there was some kind of conspiracy at Ardensis. Enough to get himself into a great deal of trouble with Mike Aspinal."

"But he couldn't tell me what that was."

"Because he said he didn't know himself. Whether that's true or not, I think that should point us back to the encrypted emails and tell us that we've been right about them. I think they're evidence of the same conspiracy that Tempest was talking about."

"What use are they if we can't read them?"

He doesn't reply straight away but I get the idea that he has more to tell me.

Breakfast is finished and he begins to clear the table. "I've been thinking about the company. The kind of structures Ardensis must have. Who the people exchanging those encrypted messages might be. We know that Aspinal and Hardman were planning something. But why would they need to send secret messages to so many others? What if Hardman and Aspinal were strong-arming key people at Ardensis? It's the kind of thing Hardman has done before. If that's so, there could be a way to discover their names."

"How could we do that?"

"Well, there's one thing we could try. We can't read what the messages say but in the headers we can see the email addresses. What if we send a message to those addresses and see what, if anything, comes back."

"What would it say?"

"Anything to create a response."

He opens his laptop and begins typing. "What about this?"

*Dear all*
*You'll know by now that Mike is no longer with us. But that doesn't need to stop us. The deal is still on.*
*Justin*

"They'll be alarmed that the message isn't encrypted as usual and that it's come from an email address they haven't seen before, but one or more of them might be frightened enough to reply."

I finish reading the message. "What deal?"

"I have no idea. But we know they must have been planning something."

"One of the recipients is likely to be Hardman himself."

"We can't avoid that. It's a risk worth taking. Do you agree?"

"OK. Press *send*."

He sends the message. "Don't get your hopes up, Issy. I'd rate our chances of success as low to minimal."

"If it's all we have."

He nods. "Worth a try."

His eyes turn to the screen as a message comes in.

*I'm out of the office until February 21st. I'll do my best to catch up on everything when I return.*
*Charles*

Adam gives a broad smile. "Can't believe our luck! He must have put that message on all his accounts."

I smile back. "So, who is Charles?"

"I have no idea. But now we have a name."

# CHAPTER 50

Ives finds that Lesley is again on duty early in the incident room at Lions Yard, checking progress on the trace on the Cunningham phone.

She looks up as Ives comes in.

Ives is trying and failing to hide the fact that he feels stressed. "Where is she, June?"

"She's is in Glasgow, Steve. The data's good. Still on the move, though. From what I can see, I'd say she's behaving like a typical person on the run. Thinking that all that movement will somehow put us off the scent."

"So, when can we pull her in?"

"Bill Ginley is heading up the search. I can patch you through to him."

Ives nods and Lesley passes him a headset. He waits until he receives a nod back from Lesley that he is connected. "Bill, how's it going?"

Ives and Ginley go back more than ten years. Before Ginley moved to join the Glasgow police, they'd both been rising stars of the Metropolitan force. They'd covered each other's backs at difficult crime scenes more times than they could recall. But this is no time to dwell on their past together and Ginley comes back with business-like precision. "We have her moving North out of Glasgow, Steve. Heading towards Dougarton. Do you want us to intercept?"

"Yes, Bill. Bring her in."

"OK, Steve. I'll get back to you once we have her."

Ives doesn't like waiting. Not when he needs an arrest as much as this.

He looks towards the back wall of the incident room and notices for the first time that Lesley has set up a white board and peopled it with photographs of the players in the case. There are just four. A head shot of Mike Aspinal, taken while he lay in the morgue, and photos of Issy Cunningham, Marianne French and Colin Tempest.

Ives screws up his face. "Can't see why we need this, June."

"Just being thorough, Steve. Like we always are."

He is on the point of making a cynical rejoinder but thinks better of it and, instead, turns his attention to the details of the case.

"Listen, June, I've been thinking."

She interrupts him. "You mean worrying about the case overnight instead of sleeping?"

"No, just what I said. Thinking. We need to understand how everything has changed now we know what happened to Cunningham's daughter."

"How so?"

"You see, it's altogether probable, given what Aspinal has done to her daughter, that Cunningham would have had the murder gear with her on Valentine's Eve. Waiting in the desk drawer. Ready for use. Once she plucked up enough courage to use it and when the opportunity arose."

"Makes it sound premeditated."

"How else do you explain why she was working at Ardensis under a new name? And why she agreed to go out in Soho with Aspinal. How convenient to get him drunk. Makes it all the more likely that she was planning all along to get close to the man she hated most in the whole world. The man who'd killed her daughter and got away with it."

"They could just have gone out for a drink. Millions do it."

"No, June, I don't think so. By getting up close and personal with Aspinal, she knew she could find the moment to deliver the fatal shot. What she didn't expect was that he would go so far as to rape her. That traumatised her, as you'd expect, but that didn't prevent her from going back into his office and giving him that lethal injection. She would have watched as Aspinal died, taking in the slow agony of his death, knowing this was just some small recompense for what he did to her daughter."

"Without disposing of the syringe? Placing it back in her desk drawer?"

"As I've said before, June, things hadn't gone according to plan. She'd been raped. She was disorientated and distressed. Unable to think straight. She just knew she had to kill him. She was in no fit state to worry about cleaning up after herself."

"Except for the gloves. The ones she used to avoid fingerprints. We've searched everywhere. They're nowhere to be found."

"Maybe she wiped away any fingerprints."

"Even though she was so distressed?"

Ives shifts in his seat. "We can't afford to let ourselves be hung up on that. Not when we now have the prime motive. Cunningham killed Aspinal to avenge her daughter's death. She had the means. Mary Duggan's lab is an open source of dangerous materials. She had the opportunity. The date with Aspinal, the time they spent together in his office. Admit it. It's an open and shut case."

"Maybe, Steve. Maybe."

Ives knows that this is the closest Lesley will come to saying that he is right.

Lesley turns her attention back to her screen. "Bill Ginley's back online."

Ives prepares himself for the good news. "Tell me you have her, Bill."

Ginley sounds sheepish. "We tracked the signal along the Strathblane Road until it stopped."

"So, you have her?"

"Not yet, Steve. The tracker trace stopped moving and then went dead. When we reached the location we found out why. We're looking out at Craigmaddie Reservoir. Ninety feet of water."

"You're not saying the phone is down there?"

"That's where the trace took us before it stopped. We can try to retrieve it but my guess is that's going to be time consuming and difficult."

*Time consuming and difficult.* Ives knows this means it's not going to happen.

"So, Bill, you still have contact with the vehicle, the one Cunningham was travelling in?"

"Yes, we continued visual tracking of that, Steve. Pulled them over. But there's no sign of your suspect. Just a local man and his wife out for an afternoon at Mugdock Country Park."

"But you asked them about Cunningham?"

"Of course, Steve. They deny any knowledge of her."

"She could have left them and be on the run. What's the terrain like out there?"

"Countryside, trees, golf courses. I have men out there searching."

Lesley waves to direct Ives to another screen further down the incident room. "You need to see this, Steve."

She points to security camera footage of a couple walking under a large multi-coloured umbrella. "They're walking along Cornwall Road in Ruislip."

Ives shrugs. "So what?"

"Wait while I run it forward. You see, just here as they stop to go up to one of the houses. They think the umbrella is shielding them from the camera. But just here, the umbrella slips." She pauses the playback. "And there she is."

Ives stares in disbelief. He's looking at a good likeness of Isobel Cunningham. "When was this taken, June?"

"Yesterday evening."

"And you're telling me that all the time we've been tracking the Cunningham phone in Scotland you've been looking at the London security camera footage?"

She risks a smile. "You know me, Steve. Leave nothing to chance. I had a little help. I asked Claire Benson to keep an eye on the footage for me. She did a good job. For a trainee."

Ives shakes his head and returns to the line to Scotland. "Bill. Call off the search. We have a sighting of Cunningham here in London. And make sure you detain the couple in the car for impeding a police investigation."

He closes the line. He knows he's been fooled into thinking that Cunningham ever left London.

He turns to Lesley. "What the hell was Cunningham doing in Ruislip?"

"That's what we need to find out."

"At least we know how to find her now. Look for the umbrella."

He stands and shouts back to Lesley as he leaves the room. "And don't let anyone else know we fell for this. No one. Ever."

"Yes, Steve."

"One more thing, June. Find out who did this."

# CHAPTER 51

The look of satisfaction on Adam West's face is clear to see. "I've uncovered something at Companies House, Issy."

"You mean you've found Charles?"

He smiles. "There's a Charles Noble listed as a director and Board member. If I'm right, he's the Charles that replied to our phishing email."

"So, we talk to him."

He sits beside me on the narrowboat couch. "That's not so easy. We have a name but the Companies House website is short on contact details." He pauses. "Who do you trust at Ardensis? Someone there may have had dealings with members of the Board and may be able to help us."

"There's Marianne French. If anyone knows, she will."

"Then as long as you tell her nothing about being here, contacting her is probably another risk worth taking."

"I'll be careful."

"So long as Ives carries on believing you're in Scotland, you should be safe enough."

Adam takes me to a public phone on the Commercial Road, a ten-minute walk from the Marina. We use the umbrella as a parasol to shade us from the bright sunshine and to keep our faces from any security cameras along the way.

When Marianne picks up, she's full of questions about how I am and where I've been but I tell her there's no time to answer. She tells me she understands.

SEB KIRBY

"I need information about someone on the Ardensis Board. An address for Charles Noble."

"Why would you want that?"

"I need your help. Please, Marianne."

"I'll try. Charles Noble is someone I've had to visit to drop off paperwork from time to time."

"You have an address."

"Yes, but I can only give it to you on condition that no one knows it came from me."

"Yes, of course."

She gives me the address. Markham Square, off the King's Road in Chelsea."

"I can't thank you enough, Mari."

"Just stay safe."

I close the line.

We return to the lock up to retrieve Adam's car and he drives me to meet Noble. Markham Square is one of those tranquil, genteel side streets off the King's Road where, these days, properties command a seven-figure price tag.

Adam shows me the house before driving on to find a place where he can park the car. "I'll wait here. It's just a two minute walk back to Noble's house."

He hands me a file from the back seat. He's brought with him the printouts of the messages he's hacked from Ardensis that use the Charles Noble email address. "Use this as your entrée."

I leave him and make my way back into the Square. I feel apprehensive as I climb the steps that lead up to the blue painted front door and ring the bell. I have no idea what to expect. No one home? An obstructive servant?

The door opens and there stands a white-haired man.

"Charles Noble?"

He nods. "What can I do for you?"

"Marianne French sent me with papers from Ardensis."

He offers a smile. "Come through to my office."

He leads me along the wide entrance hall to a room near the rear of the house. "I only work from home, these days. So much more civilized." He pauses. "By the way, I didn't catch your name."

I lie. "Isobel. Isobel Miller. Marianne French's PA."

Once inside he offers me a seat before a large well-ordered desk. He sits opposite me in a leather upholstered office chair and holds out his hand to let me know that he wants the papers I've brought with me.

I decide it's now time to tell him the truth. "You'll have to forgive me, Mr Noble. I don't have any papers for you. I lied to get to see you."

His manner changes. He sits bolt upright in the chair and gestures towards the door. "If you're here to sell me anything you can leave right now. And, if not, you owe me an explanation."

"It's about Justin Hardman."

Noble freezes. He can't conceal the look of anguish that has overtaken him at the mention of Hardman's name. "You're with him? You work for him?"

I shake my head. "Quite the opposite."

"How do I know that? Tell me one thing that will prove otherwise."

"If Justin Hardman wanted anything from you, do you think he'd have to send someone like me? Wouldn't he be more likely to send Frank Taylor?"

Noble shivers at the sound of that name. "OK. There's no need to bring him into this."

He looks at me long and hard. A glint of recognition shines in his eyes. "I thought I recognized you. You're the one the police are looking for. But your name's not Miller. It's Cunningham, isn't it? Isobel Cunningham."

I can see his eyes turn towards the phone on his desk. "Tell me why I shouldn't call the them."

I hand him the file containing the encrypted Charles Noble emails. "Take a look at these messages. You're part of this, aren't you?"

As he begins to leaf through the paperwork, his expression changes. "Where did you get these?"

"That doesn't matter. I know enough about what Hardman has been doing at Ardensis to be sure that you've been involved with him and, whatever happens to me, the world is going to get to know all about it."

It's a bluff. I just have to hope he won't call it.

He returns his attention to me. "All right. Tell me what you want."

"I need to know just what you're involved in."

"Why would I be involved in anything? And if I were, why would I tell you?"

I try to play further on his fears. "You know what happened to Mike Aspinal. The same could happen to you. Men like Taylor don't give any credit to the police in stopping men like him from ruining lives. Lives like yours."

I hit a nerve. The veneer of confidence is fast disappearing. His voice becomes apologetic. "I wanted to go to the police. But I had no belief they could offer protection for me and my family."

"From Hardman?"

"Yes. And Frank Taylor. He threatened everyone on the Board. Our families. My mother."

"For what?"

Noble leans forward to whisper. "What do you know about company takeovers by proxy, Ms Cunningham?"

I shake my head. "Not much."

"I'll tell you. If someone wants to take over a company there's a straightforward way to do it. You approach the board to make an offer."

"And if people don't want to sell?"

"Then you go hostile. You buy up the shares until get you 51 per cent. Then you have the company. You have control."

"So where does the proxy part come in?"

"Well, what if the current CEO has set up barriers to stop a hostile takeover taking place? Like building in an enormous compensation payment if they are replaced by any outside means. A level of compensation that would make the resulting company worthless. A so-called parachute payment. Then, there's only one way. A proxy takeover. Convince the current shareholders to vote against the current board and vote in a new CEO from within the company. No compensation payment needed."

"So, why would existing shareholders want to do that? There would have to be enough in it for them."

"Or enough pressure placed on them." Noble pauses. "I was going to keep quiet. Go along with the takeover, like the rest of the shareholders. Until I heard of Mike Aspinal's death."

"Why did that make you want to change your mind?"

"Because Aspinal was going to be the new CEO."

"And control the assets of the company."

"Hardman never told us more than he needed to about the deal he'd cooked up with Aspinal. He didn't need to. We were being forced to do what he wanted by simple fear. But there would be rich pickings for anyone unscrupulous enough to strip the company bare. We didn't need to be told that."

"And how many were prepared to keep their heads down and go along with the takeover?"

"Half a dozen. That's all it takes. Enough to give Aspinal the majority he needed."

I stand to leave. "Take my advice Mr Noble. Go to the police. Tell them what you've just told me."

# CHAPTER 52

Ives is spending more time than he should in his office with the door closed. In principle, he's looking through the detailed case notes that have accumulated on the Aspinal murder. In practice, he's still smarting over the humiliation he feels at having engaged Bill Ginley and dozens of his men in a wild goose chase in Scotland when, all along, Isobel Cunningham, has never left London. News spreads fast in police circles. The story will already be circulating. Ives' reputation will be taking a hit and there is nothing he can do about it.

He knows he needs to shake himself out of it. He picks up the phone and calls Lesley. "Any progress?"

"I'll be with you as soon as, Steve."

When Lesley arrives, Ives can see from her upbeat expression that she's been busy.

She sits beside him. "The house in Ruislip. Cornwall Road. Guess who lives there?" She answers her own question. "Colin Tempest."

Ives raises his eyes. "Tempest. Why would Cunningham risk being spotted going to see him? She must have a very good reason to take a chance like that."

"Which must mean that Tempest is holding back on us. He's presented himself as a bit part player at best."

"Agreed, June. Let's bring him in and find out exactly what's been going on between the two of them."

Lesley smiles. "I don't want this to sound like insubordination, Steve. But aren't you taking Scotland a little too hard?"

"Who says I've been taking it hard?"

"Two hours in your room with the door shut. I'd say that counts."

"OK. It shows. What am I supposed to do about it?"

"Bill Ginley's your mate. You go right back. He'll see to it that a lid gets put on what happened."

"Others will talk."

"So, let them. When we catch Aspinal's killer, that talk will seem cheap."

Ives is beginning to climb out of the ditch that he's dug for himself. "OK, June. Where does that leave us?"

"Getting there. It's step by step, as it always is. Now the search for Cunningham centres on London again, we'll find her, given that she has reason to risk breaking cover."

"But when we catch her, you're still saying we're short on proof."

"This may help, Steve. I ran the check on Cunningham's Internet usage, as you asked. The results have just come through."

"And?"

"There's no doubt. She searched for details of death by lethal injection. On nine occasions, all in the last month. Beginning by looking at how it's used in the US as a means of execution."

"So, she'd know about potassium chloride."

Lesley nods. "Her search takes her there. And you can see how she moves from knowing about it to checking on its availability."

Ives leans back in the chair and gives his arms a stretch. "I'm surprised you're not playing this down a little more, June. You know, you could be telling me that what she's involved in is just a search for information."

"That's true. She could be. It proves nothing in itself. But, as you'll agree, in Cunningham's case, together with finding the syringe in her desk drawer, it's significant."

"I thought you'd be with her 'til the end?"

"OK, I'll admit it, I really want to believe in her. An abused woman who's been wronged. Even though you've been giving me a hard time, something about this case makes me want to trust her. Maybe it's because Aspinal was such a waste of space, thinking he could do with people as he wanted. And, yes, I know the protocol. Don't identify too much with a suspect. Especially in a murder case. The best killers know how to make themselves look vulnerable and wronged in some way. But I really want to believe in Issy

Cunningham. I want to think she's the kind of decent woman who's above all this. But I have to admit that's becoming more difficult."

Ives doesn't smile. He knows how hard it must be for Lesley to admit this. "Don't worry, June. We all get taken in more than once in this job of ours. Like me and Scotland."

Lesley nods. "Like I said, Steve, time to put that behind us."

# CHAPTER 53

As Charles Noble shows me out, I should be paying more attention to the white van reversing around Markham Square towards me. My thoughts are all with what I've learned about the takeover of Ardensis and the prospect of returning to the safety of Adam's car.

Before I can respond, the white van draws up beside me, the nearside door slides open and I'm pushed inside by someone who must have emerged unseen from the driver's side and must have run round the back of the vehicle to overpower me.

Another man of massive bulk, waiting inside, presses me down against the corrugated metal floor.

The van door is slid shut and I can hear the sound of footsteps returning to the driver's side. After a short pause, the engine is put into gear and the van begins to pull away.

I'm overtaken by the memory that fills me with such dread that I know I must draw away before it ends. Only now there is more than I've ever seen before.

*I'm back with Mike Aspinal, feeling his body pressing down on mine, trapping me, preventing any chance of movement, forcing the air from my lungs.*

*I'm hurting and in pain. He's gorged himself on the violence he's shown me. Become the beast that had been in hiding within him. Wrecked my life for a second time.*

*He deserves to die.*

*I'm crying. Collapsed on the chair at the desk in my workspace.*

*Somewhere, back in his office, Aspinal must be congratulating himself on his night's work.*

*Yes, he deserves to die. Yet I feel so weak. Do I have the strength?*

*I reach into the desk drawer and search for the drawstring tie bag in the false compartment I've made in the bottom drawer.*

*I open the bag and place the syringe on the desk. I open the bottle that holds the potassium chloride and draw the liquid into the syringe. No need to worry about air pockets. If he gets embolism along with the dose of potassium chloride, so much the better.*

*I stare at the filled syringe. Come on, Issy. You can do this. He deserves it. If you don't do this now, he'll do it again. To someone else. Others will suffer. Your chance to finish him now.*

*He deserves it for what he did to Kelly. My sweet, innocent Kelly.*

There is more, but I force myself to look away. It's not Mike Aspinal on top of me. It's one of those who've just pulled me off the street.

How can this be happening again? How could I ever have deserved this? What have I done to make myself into such a target?

I try to scream but a large hand is pressed tight over my mouth.

"Don't call out, Mrs Cunningham. This will be much less painful if you keep quiet."

I've seen the face of the huge man now holding me. It's Frank Taylor. Hardman's enforcer. The one I saw in the champagne bar. The one in the photo shown to me by Adam.

He removes his hand from my mouth.

"You're not going to rape me?"

He laughs. "No, Mrs Cunningham. We don't do that kind of thing."

I don't feel any sense of relief at what he's just said. "I know who you are."

"Do you, now?"

"Frank Taylor."

He pushes me down against the van floor in a further demonstration of his power over me. "That won't help you because you're going to have no idea where we're taking you."

He pulls my head up by the neck and begins winding a surgical bandage round my head, covering my eyes. "Now shut up and keep still."

The van makes it out of the Square and must be joining the traffic on the busy King's Road.

Adam will guess I'm in trouble when I fail to return to the car but that will be too late. I'm on my own.

I try to concentrate on what I can do. I still have my hearing. I listen to every sound as the van picks its way through the London traffic, hoping that this might give some idea about where they are taking me. I try to keep track, as best I can, of how long the journey is taking in the hope that this might give some extra clue about the destination.

My thoughts can't stop straying to how they could have known where I was. Perhaps Charles Noble was playing me along all this time and found a way of alerting them while I was waiting to leave. But why would he have been as forthcoming about what was happening at Ardensis? Another possibility forms in my mind and I can't keep it at bay, no matter how I try.

Marianne French is the only person, other than Adam, who knew I would be there.

Marianne is my friend. Why would she betray me?

My thoughts are cut short when the van comes to a halt. We haven't been travelling long. No more than ten minutes. We must still be somewhere in central London

Taylor pulls me up into a sitting position. "We're here. Time for a little talk."

He pushes me out of the van and forces me to walk over what feels like a cobbled courtyard. A door is pulled open and, inside, I'm forced to stand still while the bandage is removed.

We're in a disused office building, looted now of all but the barest of furnishings. It's the kind of place that's been earmarked for tear down and site redevelopment.

The glass-panelled door of a nearby office down a dilapidated corridor opens and there stands Justin Hardman.

"A pleasure to finally meet you, Mrs Cunningham. Do you mind if I call you Issy? It seems most people do."

Taylor makes me follow Hardman along the corridor. Inside the office, I'm made to sit on a battered office chair facing Hardman while Taylor stands guard outside.

Hardman gives a knowing smile and looks at me, hard and long.

"Not the best idea to talk to Charles Noble, was it, Issy?"

# CHAPTER 54

DS Lesley pushes open the door to Ives' office. "There's someone you should see, Steve. He's insistent. Says it's about Ardensis and it's important."

Ives looks up from the paperwork before him on his desk. "You mean you want to stop me filling in more forms? Isn't that what this job is all about? What will the Commissioner say?"

Lesley ignores his complaints. "His name is Charles Noble. Says he's a director and significant shareholder in Ardensis. Says he's had contact with Issy Cunningham."

Ives can feel his blood pressure rising. "Does everyone know where she is but us?"

"I think we should talk to him."

He gives a sigh of complaint. "So, where is he now?"

"In an interview room. Waiting for you."

Ives follows Lesley downstairs to the room and takes a seat opposite Noble.

Ives looks the man over with distaste. He is the epitome of the city gent – white hair, bright eyes, self-satisfied expression, grey Savile Row suit, blue silk handkerchief in the jacket breast pocket - the kind Ives assumes is a thing of the past. And when Noble speaks he has that clipped upper-class accent that tells of an earlier career in the Army.

"I want you to know it has taken some courage for me to come to see you like this, Inspector, and I want two assurances before I can tell you anything."

Ives smiles. "Which are?"

"I need you to treat what I have to say in absolute confidence."

"I can assure you of that."

"And I'll need police protection from me and my family."

Ives glances at Lesley, a look that says: *Police protection, that's expensive. This will need to be something important if we're going to get that past the Commissioner.*

"We'll see what we can do."

"That's not going to be good enough."

"OK. If what you have to say merits it, I'll make a strong case for protection. That's the best I can do."

Lesley gives Ives a look back that says: *I don't think he'll have much trouble in affording to pay for his own private protection.*

Noble looks resigned. "OK. I'll take that as a yes."

"If you will."

Noble leans forward. "We need to talk about company takeovers, Inspector Ives."

Ives holds up a warning hand. "Financial crime is not on my beat. But there are people here who specialize in that. Maybe you should talk to them?"

"I need to tell you what I told Ms Cunningham."

"When you met her?"

"She came to my house, Inspector. Bluffed her way in with some cock and bull story about having papers from Ardensis."

"So, what did you tell Cunningham?"

Noble begins to tell them about the plan to take over Ardensis but before he's said much he pauses and looks apologetic. "I was going to keep quiet. Go along with the takeover, like the rest of the shareholders. Until I heard of Mike Aspinal's death."

Ives shuffles in his seat. "Excuse me, Mr Noble. You don't look like the type of man who would be easily intimidated."

"You don't know the kind of people involved. A man called Taylor. Frank Taylor."

Ives shoots Lesley another glance. They know all about Frank Taylor. Son of East End hard man Charlie Taylor, Frank is known as a fixer. One who has found a ready place in the City and wealth and power way beyond that ever produced by his father's low-level protection rackets. Taylor Junior forces deals and settles debts with a ruthless violence that shocks his victims into submission. Rumour is he's climbed further up the tree and is collaborating with a City high flyer whose identity is a secret to the police. Not that, until now, this has been of much concern to Ives and Lesley.

Noble continues. "Taylor threatened us all. Our families. My mother."

"So why didn't you go to the police back then?"

"You know the answer to that, Inspector. You can't even agree protection for myself and my wife, let alone for my parents and children."

Lesley stops taking notes. "Frank Taylor is the worse of a bad lot. We know that. But tell me, are you saying that he's the brains behind a plot to take over Ardensis?"

Noble turns towards her. "No that's Hardman. Justin Hardman. He's the one who's been driving the whole thing, using Taylor to threaten people."

Ives comes back in. "What can you tell us about Hardman?"

Noble frowns. "That, in his own way, he's just as nasty a piece of work as Taylor. But he's cunning and quick enough on his feet to keep himself out of the picture as much as possible, pulling the strings while people around him suffer." He pauses to remove the handkerchief from his top pocket and wipe his hands with it. "People like him shouldn't be allowed to run roughshod over the lives of law abiding citizens, Inspector. But that's just what he does and there seems to be nothing to stop him."

"Leave that to us, Mr Noble."

When Noble finishes telling them about the takeover, Ives stands and points Noble to the door. "I want to thank you for coming forward, Mr Noble. It's taken great courage to come here and speak to us today. Be assured, we'll be taking seriously all you've had to say."

As Noble leaves, Ives is quick to make his frustration known to Lesley. "How does a villain like Frank Taylor figure in this? And how is he linked to Justin Hardman?"

Lesley is already searching her laptop. "Give me an hour or so, Steve, and I'll see what I can find."

# CHAPTER 55

Through the frosted glass panel in the door, I can see the looming silhouette of Frank Taylor, standing guard outside, as Justin Hardman looks me up and down. He's eyeing his prey, savouring the moment.

"Tell me, Issy, what were you doing at Charles Noble's house?"

"You know why I was there."

"I want to hear it from you."

Since he knows already, I can find no reason not to tell him. "He told me about what was happening at Ardensis. How you've been strong-arming him."

He smiles. "That's stuff no one's supposed to know. How do you think that makes me feel?"

"How would I know?"

His eyes burn with a sudden hatred. "Issy, this is something I can't let go. You must know that."

I shiver as I realise that neither Hardman nor Taylor has shown any concern about revealing their identities to me. That means only one thing.

He changes the subject and, for a moment, the look of hatred is replaced with one of curiosity. "Tell me, Issy, why did you shack up with Mike Aspinal?"

"Why does that matter to you?"

His eyes turn for a moment towards Frank Taylor. "That won't do, Issy. You need to do better than that."

"If you must know, I was scared."

"Scared of what?"

"Of what would happen to Colin Tempest's family if I couldn't stop Mike from sacking him."

He shows his perfect, over whitened teeth in a half smile. "And why would that matter to you? He has his life, you have yours."

"I couldn't bear to think of his wife and kids being made to suffer like that. His wife's eyesight. His kid's schooling. It wasn't fair what was going to happen to them."

"So you're the caring type."

I shake my head. "Don't make it sound like that. It was about trust. Does that mean anything to you?"

"So, you trusted Tempest?"

"He needed help."

"What if I was to tell you that Colin Tempest's wife has no problem with her eyes? And his kid has no problem with her schooling. "

"I wouldn't believe you. How could you know?"

"Because I can assure you that Tempest has never been married. He has no wife and no family. He's been using you."

I feel the muscles in my stomach clench. "Why should I believe you?"

"Did you ever meet them? See any photos of them. Don't you find that strange?"

"Why would Colin do a thing like that?"

Hardman stands and begins to pace the room as he speaks. "I don't need to tell you this, but in the circumstances, perhaps I should. I think you know by now that a deal was about to go down at Ardensis, from which I stood to gain a considerable sum. Money I was owed. Well, Tempest was part of that deal. He was one of my insiders, keeping an eye on Aspinal to make sure he'd go through with the deal as planned."

"So, why did Aspinal want to sack him?"

"You still don't get it, do you Issy? Apart from me, the deal could only benefit people who were employed by the company. With Tempest off the payroll, he'd receive nothing."

"But up to that point they were in it together?"

"Of course. They were both playing ball. But then Tempest got other ideas. He wanted more than I was prepared to give him. He put the burn on Aspinal to give him more. Told him he knew

159

something about Aspinal's past. Something I think you also know, Issy."

"That he killed my daughter?"

"Yes. Tempest threatened to expose Aspinal to the world. For men like Aspinal, reputation is everything. It would have ruined him. But, of course, with Aspinal dead, that no longer matters."

"But you didn't know about it."

"No. And if I did I could have stopped it."

"So you blame Tempest?"

His eyes flare. "No, Issy, I blame you. Tempest may have found a way of skimming off from the deal but I'd have discovered that sooner or later and put that right. But the deal would have gone through. And you saw to it that didn't happen."

"You're saying I killed Aspinal?"

"Didn't you?"

"Maybe I did. I wanted to kill him for what he did to Kelly. Is that so bad?"

"So you're no angel, then, after all."

"I don't see why that's anything you'd know anything about."

He moves in close and stares right at me. "That's where you'd be making a big mistake. Wouldn't it be easy for people like you to believe that people like me are ignorant, lacking in morality. That's so far from the truth. And, you want to know why? I'll tell you. I'm owed. Big time. From way back. From when my family was cheated out of what was rightfully theirs. But I realised right from the start that if I was going get back what I'm owed, I was going to have to be the intellectual and moral equal of all those who might presume they're so much more deserving than me. Not equal, in fact, but superior."

He moves back and sits opposite me once more. "And because of that, I'm not the sort to let anything go that I don't understand. I have to know why you trusted Tempest. Why he found it so easy to take you in."

I'm hoping I can find a way to reason with him. In this moment it's the only way I can think of convincing him to let me go. So, I tell him about my mother and how I blame myself for my parents' divorce. I tell him about Kelly and how I blame myself for not taking her to the school bus. It feels like a confession. With each word I speak I realise that Hardman is the first person I've ever tried to explain this to.

Why this man, of all men? Perhaps it's because I know what he plans to do with me and that he might be the last person in the world I'll ever talk to.

He scrutinises me once more, as if he needs to make sure that what I'm telling him is real. "So, you've made a habit of torturing yourself about things that no one can change."

I'm crying now. "I guess so."

"And so, whenever someone confides in you and tells you they have a problem, you're so convinced that bad things will happen that you feel compelled to believe them and act on what they say." He laughs. "Maybe you are some kind of angel, after all."

He looks away and begins to recite something I've heard before but can't place. "But man, proud man, Drest in a little brief authority, Most ignorant of what he's most assured, His glassy essence, like an angry ape, Plays such fantastic tricks, before high heaven, As make the angels weep."

I'm playing for time, hoping he won't know it. "Mike Aspinal told me there are no such things as angels."

"Well, he's wrong. Just don't make the mistake of thinking they're always on the side of the good." A glint of fanaticism shines in his eyes. "And that's true whether you regard them as metaphorical or not."

He comes up close once more. "Don't make the mistake of thinking that you know anything about a man like me."

He glances back in the direction of Frank Taylor's silhouette. "Frank. He's an ape. Don't ever think I'm like that."

I know then that he counts himself as one doing only good, on the side of the angels, recovering what he is certain he is owed. Unaware that anything else could matter as much. "So, tell me, what makes you so sure that for one second I'd ever bother to think anything at all about a man like you. A man who thinks the world owes him a living. A man who has to see himself at the centre of everything."

He sneers. "It's not the world that owes me anything. It's those families that took from my family without ever considering that there would be consequences. Families like the Blakemores. They're the ones that owe me. They're the ones that have to pay."

"So, you have some kind of vendetta with Vince Blakemore. Your interest in Ardensis is about more than just the money. You're a dark angel driven by revenge. There's no salvation in that."

His eyes focus down to pinpoints. "I don't need saving. And if I did, salvation from what?"

I've stopped crying. I know now how to hurt him. "From yourself. From a life that's one long lie meant to hide the self-loathing that invades every last part of it. I pity you. Even if you recover every penny you think you're owed, nothing will change the cold truth that your family was a failure."

He looks away. I've hit a nerve. "So, you think you have nothing to lose, Issy Cunningham. As I told you, never underestimate a man like me."

He calls out and Frank Taylor comes in. "Frank, I think it's time you took her somewhere and did what needs to be done. She's of no more use to us."

The big man grunts his approval.

As I feared from the start, I'm sure then that they're going to kill me.

"Then why all this?"

He smiles again. "Just staying ahead of the game. There was a chance I might be missing something about what happened to Aspinal. Now I know I wasn't."

Taylor grabs me and pulls me to my feet. I have no answer to the brute force of those hands as he pushes me towards the doorway.

# CHAPTER 56

Lesley is back in Ives' office within the hour.

"Justin Hardman is a difficult man to pin down, Steve. He has a clean record. You might call it spotless. Contributes to a dozen charities and both of the main political parties. Runs his own company and is regarded as a rising star of the investment world. He's even featured in a couple glowing comment pieces in the business press."

Ives grunts. "And yet Charles Noble is telling us that Hardman is hand-in-glove with Frank Taylor."

"I agree. It doesn't add up. I can't see any reason why Noble would be inventing this. The man was genuinely in a state of fear."

"Which means that Hardman is almost certainly one of those cunning types who manages to stay just beneath the radar while the bad things that are happening around him always seem to be down to someone else. I've met his kind before."

"So, we bring him in for questioning?"

Ives shakes his head. "Not without being sure of ourselves, June. He'll bring a fancy lawyer along with him and make our lives a misery if we're seen to accuse him in any way without firm proof. I'm tempted to pass on what we know to the Business Fraud squad and leave them to investigate the accusations Noble is making. Meanwhile we have a murder case to get on with."

"But what if what Hardman was doing is material in the Aspinal killing? Surely that means we have to talk to Hardman about that?"

"OK. I take the point, June. Where do we stand with the encrypted messages that we recovered from Aspinal's computer? If they involve Hardman, that would strengthen the argument to bring him in. What's the hold up?"

"Aspinal used one of those online email encryption services. Which means we need the key to unscramble them from the encryption service company."

"So we've asked for the key?"

"We have. But that requires a court order. That could be served later today. But the company may object, citing the privacy of their users."

Ives paces the room to try to hide his frustration. "Why do these well-meaning intellectuals and free speech campaigners think they can go on standing in the way of justice?"

"Not everyone sees it in such black and white terms, Steve."

"Which means everything takes so much time."

"As these things normally go, Steve, this counts as warp speed."

"So, we wait?"

Lesley nods in agreement. "Wait to see what the messages contain and then take a decision on interviewing Hardman."

"I guess so. Anything else, June? Anything that might allow us to make progress of any kind?"

"You may want to see this, Steve." Lesley shows Ives the printout from the file she's been carrying along with her notebook.

Ives furrows his brow as he looks over the document. "Relevant?"

"Just a little, Steve. It's a timed and dated Post Office receipt for the movement of a parcel from London to Glasgow."

The hairs on the back of Ives neck begin to prickle. "Do we know the sender?"

"We do. It's a Professor Mary Duggan."

# CHAPTER 57

Vincent Blakemore kicks off his shoes. It feels strange to be here again in the CEO's chair. In this office. The place where Mike Aspinal died. Despite everything, he admits to himself, it's good to be back.

Running Ardensis was harming his health, he couldn't deny that. He'd given so much in founding the company. Keeping it on the rails had put years on him. It was better for him and for the company that he took a break. Three months in the States with his son's family was just what was required. When he came back he'd have fresh determination to take Ardensis to the next level.

At least that's the version he wanted everyone to believe. And they swallowed it whole.

In truth, there was a compelling reason to slip away. And that was Mike Aspinal.

Where to start? Vince Blakemore knows now that, much earlier, he should have discounted the reports he was receiving from Aspinal. Looking back, it should have been clear that the reports were too good. No business he was ever involved with was ever so free of problems, no matter how careful the planning. There was nothing but equanimity in Aspinal's reports. He must have been making them up.

Which all fed into the long held feeling that Mike Aspinal was too good to be true. Yes, he made a good fist of being the right hand man. Being always there when needed, no matter what the day or hour. Being dedicated to the future of the company. But there was something all too calculating about the man, a perception that Vince was unable to shake off, no matter how hard he tried.

What if Aspinal wasn't as he seems? What if the past three years they'd worked together were little more than an elaborate ploy to win his trust while all along Aspinal's personal ambition was what was fuelling their collaboration? How could it be possible to discover if Ardensis would be delivered into the right hands when Vincent stood down? These were the issues that had led him to leave.

There was only one way to tell and Vince had taken it. The trip to the States was real enough but it was made in the knowledge that he would be kept in touch with every detail of how Mike Aspinal handled himself while he was acting CEO. He had a trusted person in place who would see to that by sending a detailed account of everything that took place while Vincent was away.

So, what about his failsafe? Why hadn't he pressed the panic button? Time to talk with him.

Colin Tempest comes into the office and makes a good show of welcoming his boss back.

"Good to see you're now where you belong, Vince."

But his body language tells another story. He looks defensive, expecting the worst.

Blakemore tries not to let on about what he's thinking. "And it's good to see you, Colin. I've missed the cut and thrust of it all." He pauses. "You know why I'm back?"

Tempest nods. "What happened to Mike. It's shocked us all."

"You've been helping the police?"

"Doing what I can. DI Ives is very thorough. He's been asking a lot of questions. You know it's murder."

"Never thought anything like that would happen here. But it is what it is and we have a business to keep on track. Has it suffered?"

"The word is out about Mike but that hasn't translated into any of our clients closing their accounts."

"So, we see to it that things stay that way. I'll head up the campaign and draw up a ground plan. You'll help me implement it."

Tempest nods again. "Of course. You can depend on me."

Blakemore leans forward. "You didn't see any of this coming?"

"How do you mean?"

"You did a good job keeping me informed while I was away. Telling me about the takeover. But you didn't report much about Issy Cunningham."

Tempest shuffles in his seat. "No one could have predicted what happened between her and Mike." He pauses. "You know the police are saying that she's wanted for killing Aspinal?"

"And you believe that Issy could do a thing like that?"

"I don't know, Vince, honestly, I don't. You know Mike raped her? It seems that the evidence against her is piling up."

Blakemore stands and begins to pace the room. "We need to keep this company on the road, Colin. Make sure this thing doesn't derail us."

"Yes, Vince."

"Now's the time to tell me if there is anything else I should know about what's been happening while I've been away."

"Nothing that won't keep, Vince. Nothing that won't keep."

# CHAPTER 58

Frank Taylor bundles me out of the room and forces me to begin to climb the main staircase of the derelict office building.

He grunts as he pushes me up the stairs. "I hear the view from the roof is fine. You can see half of London from up there."

He's going to push me off. I know that. It's what Hardman would have taken great satisfaction in planning. Distressed woman found dead after falling from deserted office building. Nothing more than anyone might have expected. She's had so many problems in her life.

By the time we reach the first bend in the staircase, Taylor is starting to sound breathless. I realise that if he would just let go of me for a moment, I could outpace him up the stairs.

I pretend to stumble and turn my ankle, crouching down in pain.

He releases his grip for a moment while he reaches for something in his jacket pocket.

His gun.

But in that instant, I have a chance to break free.

I turn and bound up the stairs, reaching the next bend in the staircase before he can aim and fire.

I take the next flight of stairs two at a time, knowing that I must make it round the next bend before he has another chance to see me and fire.

There's no time to look back. I just have to hope that the sudden impact of a bullet in my back isn't going to come.

I round the next bend in the staircase with my lungs heaving but without being hit.

I know I must be increasing the distance between him and me. Taylor is big and strong but he's not a fit man.

I risk pausing and looking back. There's no sign of him. I can hear him below me, struggling to catch up, wheezing now as he struggles to get enough air in his lungs.

I'm escaping, but to where? The staircase leads only to the roof, the place where Taylor wants to take me all along.

I need to find a way out. I look around as I run up the next flight of stairs, searching for an answer.

On the wall at the top of this flight of stairs is an old fire extinguisher, left in place even though most of the building has been decommissioned. If I can just pull it off its stand, it might give me my chance.

I pull at the extinguisher. It won't move. I can hear Taylor approaching, getting ever nearer. I heave as hard as I can in one last attempt to shift the extinguisher before I have to run on.

It comes loose. It's heavy. I struggle to lift it above my head. I use all my strength to climb the first few steps round the next bend in the stairs.

I wait until Taylor is on the point of reaching the top of the flight of stairs below me before stepping down and hurling the extinguisher at him.

It catches him full in the chest and overcomes his balance. He falls back, clattering down a dozen steps, and lies there, motionless.

I don't dare approach him. What if he's just incapacitated for a moment?

I wait. He doesn't move. I tiptoe back down the stairs towards him.

The gun has fallen from his hand and is laying there, three steps below him.

I have to pass over his body to reach the gun. If he comes to as I step over him, he'll have me again.

It's a risk I have to take. The longer I wait the greater the chance he'll come round.

I hold my breath and tiptoe towards him. He doesn't move as I step over him and reach the gun.

I pick it up. I haven't held one before, let alone used one. What if it has a safety catch that I don't know about?

There is no time to think. I creep further down the stairs. I don't know where Hardman will be. Perhaps he's still in the room where they held me. Or perhaps he's outside near his vehicle, waiting for Taylor to report that he's completed his work.

As I reach the foot of the stairs, there is Hardman, pacing the building entrance, waiting for Taylor.

He's facing away from me and can't see me. If I'm silent enough, I can get close enough to use the gun.

I come up behind him and pause. "Hardman. Don't do anything. Just turn and face me."

He turns and I can see his eyes bulge as he takes in the gun pointing straight at him. "You have no idea how to use it, Issy, believe me."

I shout back. "You want to risk it?"

He raises his hands. "No need for anything silly, Issy. You're free to go, as you wish."

I move closer, indicating with the gun that he should go back into the office where they held me. "You were going to have me killed. Give me one good reason why I shouldn't finish you now?"

He turns and stares at me with pleading eyes. "Don't be like me."

I make him go inside the office and I close the door behind him.

I shout back. "Come out and I'll kill you."

I head for the open front door and begin to run.

# CHAPTER 59

It's close to impossible to conceal his anger but Stephen Ives knows he has to try.

Mary Duggan sits there looking so composed. You'd never have thought she'd been arrested and brought to the interview room at Lions Yard against her will, served with a summons that alleges the serious offences of impeding a police investigation and aiding a wanted criminal.

"So, Professor Duggan, tell me why I shouldn't have you charged right away?"

She still looks unruffled and even manages a smile. "I have no idea what you're talking about, Inspector."

"You don't deny arranging for Isobel Cunningham's phone to be transported to Glasgow with the intention of creating the misleading impression that she could be found there?"

"I do deny it, Inspector. Why would I want to do such a thing?"

"To help your friend escape a charge of murder."

"I can't imagine why you suspect me."

Ives glances at DS Lesley who is sitting beside him.

Lesley fires up a laptop computer and starts a video running, which she shows to the professor.

Ives continues.

"This is you entering Mile End post office two days ago. You don't deny it?"

Mary Duggan gives a shrug of the shoulders. "Looks like me. It's no crime to go to the Post Office, is it?"

Ives points at the laptop screen. "And here you are handing over a parcel for delivery and paying the fee."

"OK."

"A parcel that's just the right size and shape to contain a mobile phone."

"Or any other small object. So?"

"The Post Office records the time and destination of every transaction. That's how they can give you a certificate of posting." Ives pauses. "And we've checked those records and, what do you know? That parcel, your parcel, was destined for Glasgow and sent just a few hours after Cunningham disappeared from the Chelsea and Westminster."

"Glasgow?"

Ives can feel his blood pressure rising. "There's no need to play quaint, professor. That's where the Cunningham phone was traced to. Your parcel was sent to Glasgow and the Cunningham phone turns up there, apparently moving around just as you might expect if someone was deliberately trying to throw the police off the scent."

Mary Duggan remains unmoved. "You still need to show that's anything more than a coincidence."

"OK. If we're wrong in saying you sent the phone, just what did you send in that parcel?"

"A birthday present for an old school friend."

"You must know that we have the name and address of the recipient. John McDonald of Cavendish Street in the Gorbals. He could be in as much trouble as you are. Not much of a way to treat a friend?"

"I sent him a dram of twenty year old whisky. That's all I did."

Ives fakes a laugh. "Oh, come on, professor. Surely you can do better than that? Sending whisky to Scotland?"

"He's a Scot. He likes whisky. Surely that can't surprise you, Inspector?"

"And you deny asking him to carry on using the phone once he'd received it to give the impression that Cunningham was in Glasgow?"

"I have no idea what you're implying."

"That you conspired with him to mislead the police about Cunningham's whereabouts."

"That's what you might want to claim, Inspector, but you have no proof."

"And why would you say that?"

"Because you don't have the phone, do you? This is all a bluff to try to get me to confess to something you have no way of proving I was involved with. Without the phone you have no fingerprint evidence, no DNA or fibre analysis to connect me or John McDonald with what you're claiming took place. No doubt you've already spoken with John. No doubt he's corroborated everything I'm saying."

Her smile tells Ives that he is not about to gain any kind of confession from her.

He throws his hands up in despair. "Because you knew all along that the phone would never be found. Because there's zero chance of it being recovered from the bottom of Craigmaddie Reservoir, as you've planned all along."

"Say what you like, Inspector. You have no proof against me." She pauses. "And, if you don't mind, I want to leave now. Is there anything stopping me?"

He looks deep into her eyes. "I want you to think carefully before you answer this. Do you know the whereabouts of Isobel Cunningham? I have to warn you that aiding a criminal in the act of murder carries a substantial sentence."

She doesn't blink. "No, Inspector."

Ives takes deep breaths. "Don't think you won't hear more about this, professor. What if your university was to get to hear about our suspicions?"

"Is that a threat, Inspector? Sounds desperate."

Ives faces up to the inevitable need to climb down. "You're free to go. But be very clear that we'll be watching your every step. And if we are able to show you've been aiding a wanted murder suspect, know that we'll be asking for a custodial sentence."

# CHAPTER 60

Vincent Blakemore picks up the phone and dials.

When Mark Strang picks up, it's clear he's been sleeping.

"Vincent. You've called early."

"It's gone ten."

"Like I said. Early."

"We need to meet."

"Usual place, sometime after noon."

"Make it 12.00. Bring your brain with you."

As if they believed he wouldn't have someone like Strang taking care of intelligence while he was away. He wouldn't have lasted long in this business if he wasn't used to taking precautions.

This is something Hardman and people like him would never be able to understand. The reason why the Blakemore family has won, and will continue winning, is that they are ruthless. More ruthless than anyone would ever suppose.

They meet in the multi-storey car park on Tottenham Court Road.

Strang slips into the front passenger seat of Blakemore's waiting SUV. "What do you want to know, Vince?"

Blakemore is surprised that Strang needs to ask. When he'd heard that Mike Aspinal was planning to take over Ardensis behind his back, Blakemore had asked Strang to find out who else was involved.

"I need to understand if the takeover is stalled now that Mike Aspinal is no longer with us. And if it could still go ahead."

"Like I told you, that kind of information isn't easy to come by."

"You're being well paid."

"Believe me, you're getting value for money." He turns and smiles, as if expecting praise.

"Just tell me what you have."

"Well, the game is the same. Like I told you before you came back, it's a proxy takeover. Pressure on the Board. Using Aspinal as the lever. Now he's gone, there is no lever. Looks like the deal is off. Hardman certainly thinks so. He's going round telling people that he's owed."

"But he could just be saying that while finding another way to take over the company."

"Can't rule it out."

"Then, it's time to make sure that can't happen."

"That's going to cost a whole lot more."

"How much more?"

"Another hundred thou."

"OK. Just make sure the problem goes away."

# CHAPTER 61

I'm running when I know I should be walking. Escaping from the abandoned building where Frank Taylor tried to kill me.

Slow down. You'll draw attention.

Taylor's gun is still in my hand. I stop and stare down at it. It looks alien, a thing I can't imagine ever holding. I open my fingers and let it drop to the ground. It clatters on broken asphalt.

I've stopped in the centre of a disused car park, the one that must have been attached to the derelict offices that Hardman brought me to when they were still in use.

I know I'm not far enough away from them. At any moment Hardman, or one of Taylor's men he might have summoned, could be on me. I have to fight to remove from my mind the insinuating thought that I might remain here, rooted to the spot, unable to move, until they find me.

I walk on, glancing behind me every ten paces or so. No sign of them. So far.

In the distance, in the gap between two buildings, I can see and hear the roar of London traffic. If I could reach that street before they grab me again, I might be able to lose myself in the crowds that must be there.

Distances extend. Time slows. Each step takes what must be a minute and brings me just inches nearer to that busy street. And all the while there is the threat of what might be coming up behind me.

The gap between the two buildings is, in fact, a narrow alleyway. The kind of place where you could come to grief without anyone knowing, even though it's so close to the main road.

I edge along the alleyway with the sounds of the traffic on the main street ahead growing louder as I come closer.

One last look behind. No one following. Hardman must have been delayed long enough in discovering what happened to Taylor for me to get this far without being apprehended. I have to make the most of this and not lose courage now.

I make it onto the broad main street where local shoppers and tourists throng the pavements and busy themselves with all that's on offer in the prestigious stores that flank both sides of the street. So many others for whom life is being lived as open and normal, without the dread that I have come to accept is always with me.

I look up at the walls above the storefronts, searching for a street name but I can't find anything to tell me where I am. I walk on, hiding as best I can amongst the crowds.

How to escape? How to make it back to the safety of the *Diamond Matrix*?

When I went to call on Charles Noble, Adam kept my bag. He said it was safer that way and he would soon be able to return it to me. But now I'm lost and need to return, I realise that without the bag, I have nothing. No money. No way of paying a fare on train or bus.

I feel in my jacket and trouser pockets as I walk. Nothing. Except, in the trouser back pocket, a single plastic card. An Oyster travel card.

I try to recall when I last used it and whether it has any money left on it, but nothing comes.

A London bus pulls into the stop ahead of me. Passengers are piling on. I run and make it to the doors before they close and step aboard. The driver gives me a disparaging look when I fumble with the card instead of swiping it on the read pad. "Come on, duchess, we don't have all day."

I swipe the card. The machine gives a satisfied beep of recognition. The card is in funds. I find a seat and look from the window as the bus manoeuvres its way down the street. Progress is slow. I fear that one of Taylor's men might have been close enough behind me to see me get on board and is already forcing a way through the crowds to board the bus at the next stop.

Then, I see a street sign. Tottenham Court Road. I begin to realise where I am.

I'm surprised that such a busy and prestigious street could be located so close to the deserted office building where Hardman held me captive. But London is like that. In a constant state of tear down and rebuild with new prosperity side by side with an older desolation.

I need to find an underground station. I know how to get back to Adam and the *Diamond Matrix* from Limehouse station. So, the urgent need is to find a way there.

At the end of the street, I can see the Underground sign for Tottenham Court Road station. I leave the bus and go into a coffee shop close to the bus stop. I take a seat near the window and watch the station entrance and the street nearby for any sign that I've been followed this far. A waitress comes up and makes a point of saying that I can't sit without ordering a drink or something to eat. I've seen nothing in the chaos of the street outside to alert me to Hardman's men knowing I'm here. I say nothing to the waitress and prepare to leave.

I make it into the subway that leads to the station entrance. I'll have to use the card again to pass through the automatic barriers that guard the entrance. I can only hope that there are still funds available on the card.

I press the card against the reader. The barrier doesn't open. A red 'X' appears with the message: SEEK ASSISTANCE. I try again but the result is the same. A uniformed railway employee comes over and takes my card. I fear he's going to detain me. But he wipes it on his jacket sleeve and places it on the reader once more. The barrier opens, displaying a bright green tick. He smiles. "No problem, madam. It's the static."

The down escalator is steep and vertiginous. I hold on tight and make it to the platform for the Central line. Take the train to Bank. Find the DLR there. Next train in 2 minutes. Crowds of fellow passengers are filling the platform, jockeying for position but I don't mind the crush. I become anonymous amongst them.

When the train bursts into sight and screeches to a halt, I let the weight of movement around me carry me aboard. The carriage is crowded to near Tokyo levels but I feel secure amongst the crush, knowing that, as the train pulls out of the station, I'm escaping.

A young Londoner offers me his seat. It's a feature of the Underground that such courtesy is commonplace amongst the increasing number of young workers that make the city thrive. It makes me feel old, but I accept the favour and sit gratefully as the train rocks and rolls as it gathers speed.

The change at Bank station is straightforward. The DLR is waiting on the platform. I climb aboard and take a seat. I try to avoid looking round to see if I'm still being followed. Looking furtive will only attract attention. I must have lost them by now.

When the train pulls into Limehouse station, I can't stop smiling. It's a nervous overreaction, I know.

I'm just a few minutes walk away from the Marina and the safety of the *Diamond Matrix*.

# CHAPTER 62

Hardman finds Frank Taylor curled in a foetal position on the stairway. "What happened, Frank?"

The big man groans. "I never was too good on stairs, Justin."

It would soon be time to move on. Hardman knows that. Taylor has been the linchpin of his success in righting the wrongs of the past but mistakes like this, allowing Issy Cunningham to gain the upper hand, show that Taylor is beyond his best. Worse of all, he's let her take his gun. That cardinal of all sins.

Taylor has done everything to distance himself from becoming the old East End gangster that his father had been. He's been open about telling anyone who'll listen that those days are a thing of the past. But that isn't enough. In the end, Taylor *is* an old East End gangster. He was born like it and he will die like it.

But in the short term, Hardman needs him. "Let's get some young muscle around you, Frank. Take care of eventualities like this."

Taylor sits upright. "If you say so, Justin. But you know I can deal with everything."

"Like you dealt with Cunningham?"

"She had a bit of luck. It won't happen again."

"Still, we now need to find her. She knows more than she should. You're up for that?"

"Just give me a few minutes, boss. I'll be all right. We'll find her, I promise."

Hardman doesn't understand how a woman as weak as Issy Cunningham can get to him like she has. But he feels threatened by her because of more than what she knows. Somehow she's peered into his soul. What she's seen there frightens him more than anything.

# CHAPTER 63

Ives stands over Colin Tempest and thumps the interview table. "Come on, Colin. We know there's more to what was happening between you and Mike Aspinal. You might as well come clean."

"I told you, he wanted to sack me."

"As you keep saying. So, why did Issy Cunningham risk coming to visit you in Ruislip? She must have had something very important to talk you about."

"You know about that?"

Ives gives a look of disbelief. "That's why you're back here in Lions Yard, Colin. What is it you don't understand about being arrested as a material witness in a crime of murder?"

Tempest shifts in his seat. "You're not suggesting I had anything to do with Mike Aspinal's death?"

"You tell us. What's been going on between you and Aspinal that meant that Issy Cunningham had to be involved?"

"OK. You might as well know. I asked her to help. I thought she had a chance of reasoning with him, of getting him to see sense."

Ives interrupts him. "And all you told us last time we interviewed you was that you could see that Aspinal fancied her."

"Yes. But I didn't know he'd go as far as so rape her. How could I have expected that?"

"So, how did you think Cunningham might change Aspinal's mind?"

"Because she knew how much losing my job meant to me. How it would affect my wife and children. My wife is close to losing her sight. It's been hard enough to keep the family together. With no job, what chance would I have?"

Ives thumps the table again. "Bullshit, Colin. We've run a check on you. You have no family. You're a compulsive liar. Why should we believe anything you say?"

Tempest's eyes move left to right and back again. "I don't have to explain that to you, Inspector. That's my business and that's that. But, tell me, why do you have me here? Tell me why I should say another word until I have a lawyer present?"

"Because if you don't want to be accused of being an accomplice to murder, you need to start talking and talking fast." Ives pauses. "Now, for the last time, what was really going on between you and Mike Aspinal? Doesn't that involve Justin Hardman?"

"OK, it's true, I've been involved with Hardman. But then there's almost no one at Ardensis who hasn't in one way or another. That's the way he works when he wants something. He digs dirt on everyone and those he can't blackmail, he threatens."

"So, what dirt does he have on you?"

"I'm in debt. Gambling debts. Hardman now owns those debts. If I don't do what he says, he'll call them in and I'll be bankrupted. Ruined."

"So he's been using you to help him take over the company?"

"He told me if I played ball, the money I'd make would more than pay off the debts. All I had to do was make sure that nothing about what was happening would get back to Vince Blakemore. That I sent him false reports about the state of play in Ardensis."

"Blakemore was aware of what was happening. About the takeover?"

"I told him about it. It was a mistake. I asked Vince to keep it secret. Somehow, Aspinal got to find out. His solution was to sack me. That way I'd get nothing from the takeover."

"So why involve Issy Cunningham? And why not take what Aspinal was planning back to Hardman?"

"If he ever found out that I'd tipped of Vince to what was happening, Hardman would have killed me, for sure."

Ives nods. "I get that. So, why Cunningham?"

"I don't know. Just that I was desperate. I just thought something would happen."

"Something happened, all right. And a man is dead as a result of it."

# CHAPTER 64

As Adam comes to help me aboard, I can see that he's worried.

"Issy, what happened? I waited and waited and you didn't show."

I tell him about being captured by Hardman and Taylor. "They pushed me into a van, Adam. Right there in the street. No one noticed. They took me to a deserted office building, somewhere near Tottenham Court Road. Frank Taylor tried to kill me. I got away and now I'm here."

He shows me to the seat at the centre of the narrowboat. "Slow down. First, we need to make sure you're OK."

"There's no time for that, Adam. I know what they've been doing at Ardensis. And now they have all the more reason to find me. You see, Hardman didn't think it mattered. Telling me how he was planning to take over Ardensis. Not when all he along he'd decided that Frank Taylor was going to kill me. But I'm still here and now I'm that much more of a threat to them."

"Don't worry, Issy. You're safe. No one knows you're here. No one followed you, did they?"

"I don't think so. I was careful. The trains were full. I disappeared in the crowd."

Adam frowns. "You took the train?"

"How else?"

"But I had your bag for safekeeping."

"I had my Oyster card. I used that."

He looks more anxious. "We may have to worry about more than Hardman. The police will be monitoring all of your digital activity by now. That will include London Underground. People don't realise that the downside of being able to use a card to swipe your way into a journey is that anyone with clearance can access a record of who you are and where and when you travel in the whole city."

"So Ives will be on to me. He'll know where I am because I used the card?"

Adam nods. "It's almost certain. Tell me something, Issy, did you swipe out at Limehouse?"

I don't have to think. "There's no automatic barrier there but I just didn't want to walk out. I thought someone might see me and report me."

"Thousands don't bother. No one reports them. If they swipe in, the system picks them up and puts a fine on their card. But many are travelling from stations with no barriers and never swipe in in the first place. You wouldn't have been out of place."

"I didn't know that. Nor did I have time to think. So, I swiped."

Adam begins to look even more anxious. "That's going to be a problem. It means Ives will know you were on the DLR and he'll know you left at Limehouse. They'll check the security cameras around the station, and may pick you up on your way here."

"And how long will that take?"

"The whole process? Receiving the information from London Underground and checking the cameras? Could be hours. Could be a lot less than that. Depends on how many officers they have on the case." He pauses and comes to sit beside me. "It means one thing and one thing only, Issy. We have to leave as soon as we can."

"How can we leave?"

He looks around. "The boat. I keep it fuelled up and ready."

"To leave the Marina? Surely the Thames is too risky for a narrowboat?"

He smiles. "How do you think I brought it here? There's a lock that connects the Marina to the Regent's Canal. Back in the day, in Victorian times, it was a major waterway, shipping coal up the Thames and transporting it by barge to the factories further north alongside the canal. The Swing Bridge at Narrow Street was entry point for goods from all over the world and Limehouse Basin was a hub of international trade. Time has moved on and the railways soon outdid the canals but, as with so much of modern London, all that historical infrastructure has remained intact. The canal is all about recreation now, of course. But it remains a viable route out through the heart of West London and then further north to the Grand Union Canal and beyond. We can head that way."

I try to tell myself that I'm safe here aboard the narrowboat but the feeling won't stay for long. The threat of Hardman and Taylor finding me is uppermost. And now I understand that in escaping from them, I've made it much easier for Ives to locate me.

# CHAPTER 65

At last there is some positive news to lift the gloom that Ives has sunk into after the confrontation with Mary Duggan.

Lesley is certain this will raise his spirits. "Steve, we have a live location for Cunningham. Courtesy of London Underground."

Ives laughs for what seems the first time in days. "Don't tell me she was foolish enough to use a card?"

"We've tracked an Oyster card, taken out in the name of Isobel Cunningham. Point of entry: Tottenham Court Road at 2.00 PM. Point of exit: 2.35 PM at Limehouse."

"Which means she must have changed at Bank to pick up the DLR. You've requested checks on the security camera footage at Bank and Limehouse?"

"Of course, Steve. And from the cameras along the Commercial Road. The pictures are already coming in. Too many of them."

Ives follows Lesley to the incident room where, earlier, Lesley had begun searching the security camera footage from Bank Station.

Lesley offers Ives a vacant seat before another of the screens and resumes her own seat. "It's all hands to the wheel, Steve."

Ives is puzzled. "Why no footage from Limehouse station?"

"The system is down there, Steve. In need of repair. Probable cause is vandalism."

"Just what we needed. If these people only knew the real cost of the damage they were doing."

"There's footage from the Commercial Road."

Ives pulls up data taken from the camera sited close to the Costcutter on the Commercial Road. He speeds through to the required time. "2.35. If she came this way there's a good chance we can track her."

They work in silence that is first broken by Lesley. "I think this is her, sir. Coming down the stairway from the Central line platform at Bank to take the DLR."

Ives comes over to the monitor and looks carefully at the image that Lesley has paused there. "Well done! That's her! No hat. Not much attempt to cover her face. Should make it that much easier to pick her out from the Commercial Road cameras."

Lesley calls up footage from further along the Commercial Road. "If she turned in the other direction and headed towards Narrow Street, this should pick her up."

They search their screens, playing through the footage for the next thirty minutes and find nothing.

Ives presses his hands together. "Where did she go, June? Why have we missed her? She wouldn't have stayed in the station once she'd swiped out. There must be some reason why she chose that station. Otherwise, why go there?"

"The cameras in that stretch don't cover everything, Steve. She may have been lucky and found all the dead spots along the route."

"OK. I want to see security camera footage from all the stores and cafes along the Road. If she passed by, we may see her." He pauses. "And I want officers out there, searching all and any locations within a half mile of the station. Something tells me she's gone to ground no further away than that."

# CHAPTER 66

There is bad news when Adam returns from the Harbourmaster's office. "They'll allow us to open the Commercial Road lock to the Regent's Canal but there's going to be a delay of two hours."

"Two hours?"

"At the least. It's to do with the way they manage the flow of boats in and out of the Marina. They give priority to the ocean going vessels when they open the Swing Bridge and main lock to the Thames. All narrowboat movements are suspended while those vessels leave. It's a matter of safety in a congested waterway."

"You didn't say our leaving was an emergency?"

"I tried. But what kind of emergency can you give for a narrowboat to need to take a trip along a canal? Meanwhile, the timing is all with the ocean-going boats. The gateway to the Thames and the lock that operates to allow them to enter the river can only be used at high tide. If they miss that, they have to wait twelve hours for the next high tide. Six vessels want to leave. They have priority over us, I'm afraid. There's nothing we can do about it."

"We could make a run for it. Take a chance. Operate the canal lock ourselves."

"And have the Harbourmaster report that to the police? I don't think we should do that."

"Or we could leave the boat and run."

"The police will have increased surveillance on every security camera in a five mile radius. We're safer staying right here."

I know he's right. "So we have to wait?"

He looks down. "Yes, until we get the all clear that we can leave."

We sit in silence for a long time, knowing that we will have to hope that neither Hardman and Taylor nor Ives will find us before we can make our escape.

Adam breaks the silence. "Issy, you need to let me know in detail what Hardman told you about what he had planned for Ardensis."

An hour passes as I tell Adam what I learned from Charles Noble.

He questions everything and returns to his computer at every opportunity to cross-reference each detail. I know what he's doing. He's being as skilful as he can in drawing attention away from the fact that time has slowed down for us as we wait for the signal that the lock to the Regent's Canal is available.

"There's one more thing you need to know, Adam. What Hardman had planned for Ardensis was not just about money. It was personal."

He looks surprised. "How come?"

"I don't think that Hardman meant to tell me. Perhaps he didn't care what he told me since he'd already made up his mind to have me killed. It kind of came out when he was trying to find out what I knew. He has a grudge against the Blakemore family. Claims they took money from the Hardmans years ago. But it's something Hardman is not prepared to forget. The takeover is as much about revenge as it is about money."

"You're saying Hardman targeted Ardensis because Vince Blakemore is the CEO?"

"That's the way it is."

"And where is Blakemore now? We should find a way to talk to him."

"As far as I know, he's still in the States."

We fall silent again as Adam begins searching online for anything he can find about links between the Hardman and Blakemore families.

I can't wait any longer to ask. "What time is it, Adam?"

He pretends not to hear. "There's nothing here I can find that tells us anything more about why Hardman should be so bent on revenge against the Blakemores. I'll need to dig deeper."

"Adam, I need to know."

191

He looks up from the screen. "OK. It's 5.00. That means we still have at least another hour to wait."

"The ocean-going boats, they're preparing to leave?"

He stands and looks out of the window. "Yes. They're manoeuvring just as would be expected for a 6.00 exit. We just have to be patient." He pauses, seeing something out there, and I can see the colour drain from his face. "It's the police."

I join him at the window and peer down the slipway, towards the Commercial Road entrance. Two uniformed officers are approaching, stopping to check each of the narrowboats moored in this section of the Marina.

Adam points me towards the stern of the boat. "It's a random check. Otherwise they wouldn't be stopping at each boat. Wait in the galley. When they come, let me deal with them."

I hide in the galley and listen to what is happening as Adam responds to the police as they request to come aboard.

"Care to give us a name, sir?"

"Brian. Brian Wilson. How can I help?"

"We're checking all the boats. Mind if we come aboard?"

Adam sounds threatened but is holding his nerve. "Checking for what?"

"There's a suspect in a serious crime believed to be in the area. We just need to eliminate any potential hiding places."

"I see."

"So, you're not going to mind us looking your vessel over?"

"There's no need. I can assure you there's no one here but me."

"All the same, Mr Wilson, we'll need to check that out."

"You're not prepared to take my word for it?"

"Sorry, sir. We need to come aboard and see for ourselves."

"What if I say no."

"Then we'd have to give some thought as to why you might want to say that. Like, why would you do that if you have nothing to hide?"

"I don't have anything to hide. But I still don't want you coming aboard."

"Very well, Mr Wilson. We'll be back. And with a warrant next time."

I come out of hiding as I hear them moving on to ask questions of the owner of the next boat along the jetty.

Adam looks shaken. "It doesn't get any easier. Standing up to authority. But that's what you so often need to do."

I feel proud of the way he's stood up for me. "You don't know how grateful I am."

He interrupts. "They'll be back. Next time with a warrant and I won't be able to stop them."

"How long have we got?"

"Hard to say. It depends on how easy it's going to be for them to get access to a judge to issue the warrant."

"Enough time for us to escape?"

He looks at his watch. "We can start to head for the canal lock in under an hour. That's if all goes according to plan with the ocean going boats leaving for the Thames. After that we'll need time to operate the Commercial Road lock itself and navigate into the Regent's Canal waterway. I can't tell you if we'll have enough time for that."

I look from the window at the boats circling the Marina in readiness for their journey along the Thames and will them to make their exit without any hitch.

# CHAPTER 67

Frank Taylor brings good news. "Justin. We've found her."

Hardman looks up. "The Cunningham woman?"

"The bitch. You've heard of Gerry Bowen. Does driving work for me. Lives on Limehouse Basin. Well, he has a narrowboat that's just three bays down from a geezer called Adam West."

"And?"

"Cunningham is hiding there. With West. He's seen them together."

Hardman is pleased. He can't shake off, how Isobel Cunningham disconcerts him far more than any of the hard cases that come into his life. Taylor will take care of them. Cunningham has dug deep in some way he doesn't want to understand. He doesn't like the fact that this leaves him with the feeling that, where she's concerned, he's not in control.

He smiles. "Then, let's finish what we started, Frank."

"No rush, boss. Finish your meal. Gerry is keeping a watch on the West boat and will keep in touch." Taylor shows Hardman the message stream on his phone. "Gerry has word from the Harbourmaster's office that West is booked to leave the Marina at 6.00."

Hardman looks at his watch. "Five-twenty now. Get some men over there."

Taylor holds up his hands. "I'd like to deal with this myself, Justin. After what happened. You understand?"

"OK. We'll have time to get over there?"

"Twenty minutes, boss. Fifteen if we take your car."

Hardman savours the moment. Isobel Cunningham would be out of the picture. The price would be paid for what he had lost. He would be in control again.

# CHAPTER 68

Lesley looks up from her screen and shouts. "I think we have something, Steve."

Ives, sitting at the screen next to her, stands to look over her shoulder. "Tell me this is good news."

"Well, we have a report from one of our team going house to house around Limehouse Station and along the Commercial Road. A young guy in one of the narrowboats moored at the Limehouse Basin Marina wouldn't let the officer aboard. Told him he should come back with a warrant. Gave the officer a false name."

Ives grumbles like a man who was tired of raised expectations that then turn into disappointment. "So, how do we know it was false?"

She points to the head and shoulders image on her screen. "Because the camera record from the officer's jacket picked up this image of the boat owner, the guy who refused. I ran it through facial recognition and this is what came back. The man in question is not Brian Wilson, as he claimed. He's Adam West."

"And he's known to us from where?"

"From his student activism days. He was arrested twice for affray on demonstrations against spending cuts."

"So he has a record and he's just the kind to insist on what he'd call his rights in not letting us search his boat without a warrant. And, from the false name he gave, he has a thing about the Beach Boys. How far does that take us?"

Lesley continues. "Just this. Adam West studied Chemistry at University of London. His professor was Mary Duggan."

Ives hugs Lesley. "That's where Cunningham must be! I'd bet my pension on it. Great work June!"

"Shall I get a team over to the Marina?"

"Yes, of course! But nothing's going to stop me going over there and arresting Cunningham myself."

# CHAPTER 69

I can't wait any longer.

"What time is it, Adam?"

He looks at his phone. "It's only five minutes since you last asked, Issy."

"But what is it?"

"Ten minutes to six."

"Sorry. It's just the feeling that Hardman and Taylor are closing in on us. Or the police are returning with a warrant. We're so vulnerable here."

Adam risks a smile. "Try not to worry, Issy. The lock to the Regent's Canal will be available to us in ten minutes. I don't see any reason for a delay. The vessels heading for the Thames are out of our way now and the Swing Bridge will be opening in a few minutes so they can leave and on time. It's a question of waiting just a little longer."

"But, once we have clearance, how long will it take to operate the Regent's Canal lock? Don't you have to fill it with water? Won't that take more time?"

"Yes. But it only takes about ten minutes. Then we'll be away."

"It can't come soon enough, Adam."

"OK. What we can do, now the waterway around us is clear, is to head over towards the lock."

I feel a wave of relief at the idea that we can at last be on the move.

I go with Adam to the stern where the tiny engine room is situated. There's just enough room for him to reach in and turn the ignition key.

The old diesel doesn't fire.

I shout out. "When did the engine last work, Adam?"

He calls back. "I checked it a week ago. It was fine then. There's no reason why it shouldn't fire now."

He turns the ignition again but with the same result. "I don't understand why it won't start. I need to check it over."

"How long will it take?"

"I can't say. Could be the battery. Or a fault with the solenoid."

I leave him to his work and walk back to the galley. I feel like crying.

Maybe I should leave the boat and make a run for it, back up to the Commercial Road or along the walkway along the Thames. I might find a way to escape.

Then I hear the sound of the old diesel engine sputtering into life and then breaking into the rhythmical pop, pop, popping that means we have power enough to allow us to leave this place.

Adam appears, a smudge of oil on his cheek. "A loose battery connection, that's what it was."

"We can go?"

"Yes. And by the time we get to the lock, it should be available."

He returns to the stern, puts the engine in gear, opens the throttle and the boat begins to move forward.

I follow him and watch as he pulls on the tiller to steer us towards the lock at the entrance to the Regent's Canal.

He shouts to be heard above the noise of the engine. "I'm going to need your help to operate the lock gates."

I shake my head. "I have no idea how they work."

"Doesn't matter. I'll tell you what to do."

# CHAPTER 70

The two men walk out to Hardman's Porsche and take their places. Taylor needs to squeeze up in the front passenger seat even though the space around him would have been adequate for most.

It will give them both satisfaction to see Cunningham die.

Hardman presses the ignition.

Unexpected silence.

The engine has not fired into life as it always does.

That means one thing.

They should get out of the car and get out quick.

Time slows down for Hardman. A slew of disconnected thoughts runs through his mind.

His distant family living well with the wealth of slaves. The sweet warmth and smells of the sugar plantation. The far off sound of the cracking of whips.

The high times when his family was the toast of Bristol, endowing libraries, donating art works collected from all over the world.

His father, the loser, telling him he would never succeed, that he should accept that this was all he should ever expect.

The fear in the eyes of the first man he ordered to be killed.

The sighs of pleasure of the many women he has attracted into his life. A procession of beautiful faces and bodies all wanting a share of the wealth he has returned to his family

In the deserted office building with Cunningham. Looking into those accusing eyes. Telling her that he knows about angels.

Why is he thinking about angels?

There is no time to move.

The car explodes in a riot and detonation of sound and destruction.

The bomb leaves a six-foot deep crater in the road beneath.

# CHAPTER 71

Ives pounds the dashboard of the police car with his fist. "Why can't the damn fools pull over?"

They've been making good progress through the London traffic, nearing the approach to the Commercial Road, but are now stalled at the junction on Whitechapel High Street, not far from Aldgate East Station.

Lesley, who is driving, turns off the siren. "There's not much they can do until the lights change, Steve. There's nowhere for them to pull over."

"One day this city will find a way to live with itself. 'Til then, we all suffer." He takes a deep breath. "So who was the officer who flagged up Adam West at the Marina?"

"Pilkington."

Ives opens his eyes wide in disbelief. "Clive Pilkington. Does he ever get out of our hair? So, he'll be there to show us to right boat?"

"'Fraid not, Steve. I tried to call him but he's off duty. We'll need to call at the Harbourmaster's Office on Goodhart Place first."

As the lights change, Lesley turns on the siren again as they force their way through the junction and onto the Commercial Road. She points to the satnav display in the dashboard. "Not sure how close we can get to Goodhart Place by car, Steve. Looks like much of the surrounding area is pedestrianized."

Ives can see where she's pointing. "You mean *gentrified*, June. Looks like we'll have to pull up on Northey Street and do the rest on foot." He pauses. "And, June, when you're driving at ninety and terrorising the locals, please keep your eyes on the road."

"OK, Steve. I never knew you were contemplating a long and uneventful life in the Metropolitan force. I completely understand."

She pulls the police car over to the right and powers across the next junction, leaving startled drivers of passing vehicles in their wake.

She shouts back before Ives can complain. "So, to get to Northey Road, we need to take this sharp right down Branch Road."

Lesley pulls the car up at the end of the road, facing the line of concrete bollards that mark the beginning of the pedestrianized area.

They leave their vehicle and begin to run along the walkways, past the smart apartment blocks that in twenty years have transformed the area from a run down afterthought of a bygone era into one of the most desirable new inner city developments.

Reaching the smart, glass-fronted Harbourmaster's Office, both are out of breath but, if they were ever to admit it, enjoying the chase.

Ives shows his badge to the young woman with the bobbed hair at the information desk. "Adam West. Where is his boat?"

She takes time to connect to the urgency that Ives is expecting. She turns to her screen. "Let me see. Mr West. Oh, yes. *The Diamond Matrix*. Here it is."

She looks back, offering an unspoken apology. "The Harbourmaster's record shows that Mr West and his boat left the Marina fifteen minutes ago."

Ives looks her straight in the eye. "I want you to get someone to show us where they've gone. Not in a few minutes. Right now."

# CHAPTER 72

"How fast can we go, Adam?"

It's a relief that we have escaped the Marina. But the *Diamond Matrix* is allowing only slow progress along the Regent's Canal and I'm sure we will be followed.

Adam calls back from the stern. "The canal speed limit is four miles per hour. Most boats do only three. I can push it to five, but that's as good as it gets. These vessels aren't built for speed."

It was a straightforward, if time consuming, business negotiating the lock at the entrance to the canal. The narrowboat had to be raised to the same height as the canal if we were to go any further. I acted as crew while Adam steered. I opened the bottom gate to allow us to enter the lock and then I used the cranked handle - the one Adam called a windlass - to open the paddles and let the water in. As the incoming water lifted the boat with agonising slowness, I couldn't stop thinking that either Hardman or Ives was right behind us.

Yet here we are, making our slow escape through the East End, the busy roadways above standing in sharp contrast to the seclusion of the waterway as it winds its way below, unseen and unnoticed.

I go to the stern to be closer to Adam. "Where are we?"

"The canal winds it's way right through this part of the city." He looks towards the park to his right. "That's Mile End Park. In a few minutes we'll pass close to Queen Mary University."

If the worst happens, I plan to jump from the boat and make a run for it along the network of surrounding streets. My fight or flight response must have been all too apparent to Adam. He seeks to calm me. "Stay out of sight, Issy. Unless you're spotted, there's every chance we can slip away."

I go back inside and sit down on the couch. Adam is right. I need to stay calm. Escaping from Hardman has left me in a heightened state of alert that, in itself, is enough to give me away.

As I look through the window at the passing canal side scene, my thoughts drift.

I'm back there at Ardensis that night. The night Mike raped me.

*He's gorged himself on the violence he's shown me. Become the beast that had been in hiding within him. Wrecked my life for a second time.*

*He deserves to die.*

*I'm crying. Collapsed on the chair at the desk in my workspace.*

*Somewhere, back in his office, Aspinal must be congratulating himself on his night's work.*

*Yes, he deserves to die. Yet I feel so weak.*

*I reach into the desk drawer and search for the drawstring tie bag in the false compartment I've made in the bottom drawer.*

*I open the bag and place the syringe on the desk. I open the bottle that holds the potassium chloride and draw the liquid into the syringe. No need to worry about air pockets. If he gets embolism along with the dose of potassium chloride, so much the better.*

*I stare at the filled syringe. Come on, Issy. You can do this. If you don't do this now, he'll do it again. To someone else. Others will suffer. It's your chance to finish him now.*

*He deserves it for what he did to Kelly. My sweet, innocent Kelly.*

*You only have to go back to the office. Make some excuse. He'll be disarmed by his success. Get close enough to him. Spike him with the needle. Push in the liquid. Watch him contort and convulse. Spit on him as he dies.*

I shake my head and look about.

Is this me?

Can this be me?

I'm aware that I'm still looking out through the window and tell myself that what matters is the here and now. On the *Diamond Matrix*. I tell myself I have to kick these thoughts away, keep them from overwhelming me.

I stand and make my way to the stern where Adam is still at the tiller, steering the narrowboat on its slow progress.

"Are you all right, Issy? You look shaken."

"It's just thoughts about all that's happened, Adam. Thoughts I have to struggle to control."

Adam stops and looks away.

We're passing under a bridge beneath the roadway above. He reaches forward to put the engine into neutral before climbing into the engine room and turning off the ignition. The engine dies.

We are in silence.

I give Adam a look that says: *why have you decided to halt the boat here, out of sight from above?*

He understands. "I heard a police car siren approaching. I thought it would continue on. But it stopped. Issy, they're right above us."

"What do we do?"

"We wait here."

But I know what this means. Ives must know about the *Diamond Matrix*. My fears are real. He's this close to finding me. "Do you think they know we're here?"

"I don't know. We have to hope they haven't seen us."

We wait and listen. Adam is whispering now. "If they saw us coming along the canal, they'd have been down here by now. My guess is they were sent to wait on the bridge and keep lookout on the canal to see if we were coming. But we made it into the tunnel just before they arrived."

"But if we leave they'll see us?"

"I think so."

"So, what can we do? If another boat comes along in front or behind us we'll have to come out or cause a hold up and that's bound to mean we'll get spotted."

Adam nods. "The canal's not too busy at the moment, but you're right, that could happen at any time."

I realise there's no point in just waiting. "If I leave the boat, where can I go?"

"You're sure you want to do this, Issy? Giving yourself up to the police might not be the worst outcome."

I know what he means. At least this would save me from Hardman and Taylor. But I want to go on. Once Ives has me, there will be little chance of coming to terms with what has happened. For good or bad, I want to be sure about what I've done after Mike Aspinal attacked me. And I need to do this on my own terms.

"I'll take my chance, Adam."

He gives me a hug. It means a lot to me, knowing as I now do that, for him, this is not easy. "Slip off the boat, Issy. Wait under the tunnel. I'll start the engines and pull the *Matrix* out into view. When they come after me, make your way back along the towpath. After about a hundred yards, you'll find stairs that lead up to the street."

I hug him back and step down from the boat, crouching on the narrow tunnel footpath. I watch as Adam starts the narrowboat and pulls out of the tunnel.

As soon as the *Diamond Matrix* comes into sight, sirens sound from the bridge above as the officers there notice it. A voice from a megaphone shouts: "Stop!"

Adam carries on.

I wait until I can see them boarding the narrowboat before I make my move, walking back along the towpath, looking out for the stairs to the street that Adam has told me about.

Have they left a lookout to cover the canal on my side of the bridge? Or has all their attention shifted to the side where Adam has taken the boat? As I creep away, I can only hope this is the case.

I reach the stairs without being stopped and begin to climb them. There's no one waiting at the top.

I keep my head down as I walk out onto the street and into the Mile End.

# CHAPTER 73

Stephen Ives climbs aboard the *Diamond Matrix* and looks around.

A slender, short-haired man sits on the couch at the centre of the boat, working at a laptop computer. He shows no concern, rather a hint of curiosity, as he glances back.

Ives comes closer. "Adam West?"

"That's me. You are?"

"No need to play games with me, Adam. You know exactly who I am and why I'm here." He pauses. "Where is she?"

"Who do you mean?"

Ives shakes his head. "You are aware, aren't you, that aiding someone suspected of a serious crime to avoid arrest is a serious offence in itself?"

"I don't get the relevance, Inspector."

"Issy Cunningham. We know you've been harbouring her. I need to search the boat."

"Only if you have a warrant."

Ives pulls a piece of paper from his breast pocket and waves it. "Which I have here."

DS Lesley climbs aboard and they search the vessel. It doesn't take long. Issy Cunningham is nowhere to be found.

Ives returns to Adam West, who is again preoccupied with his computer.

Ives is angry now and failing to hide it. "Look, we know she was on this boat when it left Limehouse. Where is she now?"

Adam gives a shrug. "I have no idea what or who you're talking about."

"In which case, I'm going to have to arrest you for obstructing a police investigation."

Ives gestures for Adam to stand and reaches forward to take his man by the arm.

Adam pulls away. "Not resisting, Inspector. Just letting you know that someone's got to move this boat to a secure place, that's all."

"OK. We'll stay while you do that."

He smiles. "And I need a phone call."

Ives scoffs. "What, so you can contact your mentor, Mary Duggan?"

"Something you might not understand, Inspector. So I can exercise my rights."

# CHAPTER 74

I make it to Mile End Station without being stopped.

I now know the risk, but I decide to use the Oyster card again.

I know Adam would have objected but, above all, I need to place as much distance as possible between myself and those chasing me. The Underground is the best way of doing this.

Adam will be questioned by Ives. But I have confidence that he will handle himself well and give nothing away.

There's a safety, an anonymity, about standing amongst the crowd of passengers as we rock and roll as the train speeds on its way out of the station.

I find my thoughts turning to Marianne. Was she the one who betrayed me to Hardman? It must have been her. Noble didn't have time to summon the white van. It was waiting as soon as I left Noble's house.

She's my friend. Why would she give me up to Hardman?

I stare at the underground map on the carriage wall above me. I'm on the Central Line, heading for Bank. From there I can catch a train to Old Street. Marianne should be at work at Ardensis. I plan to confront her. Ask her to explain what she's done.

This may not be the best-planned escape. I know this. But in this moment, more than anything else in the world, I need to know why Marianne has betrayed me.

I change at Bank and thread my way along the complex of tunnels and escalators that lead to the Northern Line.

Three minutes to wait for the next train.

There are so many security cameras down here that it's pointless trying to hide from them. Yet I keep my head down. My hope is that it will take Ives and his team too long to access the wealth of data being collected. By the time they locate me on their system, I'll have moved on.

The train arrives. It's less crowded. I will be more visible. I make for the carriage with the most passengers and step aboard.

It's a mistake.

I hadn't seen them. Two special constables must have boarded the same carriage lower down the platform. The doors are now closed. The train pulls away and I can only watch as the two officers begin to make their way through the carriage towards me.

There's nowhere to go.

I take a seat, look down and wait for the inevitable tap on the shoulder.

They come closer and I tense.

The train pulls into the next station. The doors open. The two officers step out of the carriage.

They must be on a routine patrol, the kind designed to deter terrorism.

I take deep breaths. They weren't looking for me.

At Old Street I find a public phone and call Marianne.

Just like last time, she sounds shocked to hear from me. "Issy, we've all been so concerned about you."

"Listen, Mari. We need to meet."

"Of course. When?"

"Now. Right now. I have something to ask you that won't wait."

"Shouldn't you be talking to the police?"

"There's going to be time enough for that." I pause. "If our friendship means anything, you'll agree to meet me."

"I would if I could, Issy. I'm at work."

"Make an excuse. Meet me in the coffee bar on Leonard Street."

I close the line. There could be surveillance on or around the phone box. Those who Ives has searching the camera feeds for me could be on the point of locating me.

It's a short walk to the coffee bar. I buy an Americano at the counter, find a seat in a quiet corner near the back and wait.

I don't know if Mari will come.

I give a wave as she appears at the counter. She orders and comes to sit opposite me.

"Why did you sell me out to Hardman, Mari?"

She tries to deny it. "I don't know what you're getting at."

"It had to be you. Why did you do it? Why would you treat a friend like that?"

She moves closer and lowers her voice. "I'm sorry, Issy. So sorry for what I did. Hardman discovered things about me that no one should ever know. He threatened to tell my mother. It would have killed her. He made me tell him where you were."

"You're telling me this now. Why not then?"

"Because then Hardman had me in his grip."

"So, what's changed?"

She raises her eyebrows. "Don't you know? Harman's been killed. Along with his main man, Frank Taylor. A gangland killing, they say. A bomb under their car."

"And now you're free of him?"

There are tears in Marianne's eyes. "Yes, Issy, for the first time in months. It feels like years."

I can see the real pain in her eyes. I reach out and hold her hand. "I don't care what he had on you, Mari. I don't want to know. You should keep that as your secret. I'm just pleased that we can trust each other again."

She draws her hand away. "There's something else I have to tell you, Issy. Something that may have caused you more harm than I ever thought it would."

I struggle to understand what she's telling me. "Something more?"

"I saw it, Issy. The syringe in your desk drawer. While you were out to buy lunch one day. I needed a stapler. No one uses staplers these days but the sheaf of papers I was working on needed one. I thought, who's most likely to have kept such a thing and I knew that would be you. So, I looked in your desk drawers and, when I couldn't find one, I dug a little deeper, and I found it. There in a drawstring bag. A syringe together with a bottle of clear liquid. I put it back. I didn't want you to know I'd been rummaging through your things, so I didn't mention it to you."

I can see where this is going. "So, who did you mention it to?"

"Colin. Colin Tempest."

My heart sinks. I already know how he's deceived me.

There's a disturbance near the coffee bar counter. A uniformed officer, followed by a taller one in plain clothes, brushes aside the line of customers waiting to order.

It's DI Ives come to arrest me.

I have time to glance back towards Marianne. Has she betrayed me again?

Or have they been able to track me here?

She shakes her head. I don't know if I should believe her.

I look for a way out of the back of the coffee bar but can't find one.

Ives comes up close and places his hand on my shoulder. "Isobel Cunningham. You've led us a merry chase."

# CHAPTER 75

Marianne French has been at Lions Yard police station for almost an hour, taken there as a material witness when Issy Cunningham was arrested. Issy has been led away for questioning, leaving Marianne to sit and wait.

She approaches the sergeant's desk for the third time. "When can I speak to DI Ives?"

The sergeant takes time to respond. "Like I told you last time you asked. He's unavailable right now."

"So, when does he become available?"

"I can't say."

"Is there anyone else I can see?"

He looks at the screen beside him. "DS Lesley may be able to see you."

Marianne nods.

The sergeant makes a call and motions Marianne to step forward. He walks her to a room at the rear of the station where Lesley is waiting.

The detective sergeant looks up as Marianne comes in. "Apologies for the wait."

Marianne takes the seat offered. "I need to know why you have me here."

"Let's take this from the start, shall we. Why was Issy Cunningham so keen to talk to you that she would to risk being discovered? Why were you with her?"

"She wanted to know if we are still friends."

Lesley shakes her head. "Not much of a reason to risk everything."

"It was to her. And to me."

"So, you let her down. How did that happen?"

Marianne takes a deep breath. This is something she should have told them when she was first interviewed but it wasn't possible then. Hardman still had her in his grip. She knew that Hardman was involved in some way in the events that led to Aspinal's death but she didn't know how. The fear of exposure was so great that she decided to keep quiet. But now that Hardman is gone, as she told Issy, she is free to step forward.

She begins with a flutter in her voice. "There's something I should have told you."

"About the Aspinal killing?"

Marianne nods. "I knew about the syringe hidden in Issy's desk drawer long before you found it."

"You discovered it?"

"In the bottom of the drawer, inside the drawstring bag. I found it when I was looking for something else. I still don't know why I decided to open it. Misplaced curiosity, I guess."

"Just to be clear, Marianne. When did you do this? When you opened the bag, this was how many days before Mike Aspinal died?"

"It must have been five, no six days before the murder."

"Did you tell anyone?"

"I had no idea why it was there."

Lesley looks up from her notes. "This is important. Did you tell anyone?"

"I did. I know it must have been a mistake. I told Colin Tempest."

"And what did he say?"

"He just shrugged and said nothing. But I saw his look of recognition that I'd told him something that was important to him."

# CHAPTER 76

A uniformed officer shows me into the interview room where DI Ives is waiting. She leaves me there with him. But I know there must be others watching through the large two-way mirror on the far wall.

He makes a half-hearted attempt to try to sound helpful.

"Please take a seat, Issy. I'm sorry we've had to bring you here like this, after all you've been through. But there are questions you need to answer."

I sit down and say nothing.

"Before we start, I'm required to issue a caution. You have the right to remain silent. Anything you say may be used as evidence against you. Failure to reply may be taken into account. Do you understand?"

I nod.

"Running away like that. Why did you do it? If you have nothing to hide, why didn't you want to talk to us?"

When again I don't reply, he waits.

The silence becomes overwhelming. I give in and began to speak. "I just needed some time and space to work out what was happening, that's all."

"For more than two days? What were you doing? Trying to get your story straight?"

"There are things I can't recall. I thought you knew that."

Ives raises his eyebrows in mock surprise. "I thought you'd be over that by now. Mr Mortimer certainly thinks you should be."

"Why not let me be the judge of that?"

He smiles. "It's not that simple, Issy. You see, there's the murder. You're the last person to see Mike Aspinal alive. We need to know what happened."

"I'll tell you everything I can."

Ives leans back in his chair. "OK. Let's talk about you and Mike Aspinal. You went out drinking with him in Soho on Valentine's Eve. Why did you do that? And don't say it was because he asked you and you felt sorry for him because we already know it wasn't like that."

"I was trying to help someone. Colin Tempest. Aspinal was about to sack him. I hoped to change his mind."

"It wasn't that you knew something about Aspinal that few others did?"

"What do you mean?"

"That his real name was Mark Dankworth. And that he was the one who killed your daughter, Kelly."

I can feel tears forming in my eyes. "You know about that?"

He nods. "You must have hated him. For what he did. The way he got away with it. And, now, here he was lording it over one and all without a care in the world. "

"How could I be responsible for how he ran Ardensis?"

"But you do admit that you knew he was Dankworth?"

"Yes. You may as well hear it from me. I've lived with the aftermath of Kelly's death for so long, yet it still breaks my heart every time I think about her. And that's every day. I doubt you can begin to imagine how that feels, Inspector."

"You have my sympathy, be sure of that. But that doesn't alter the fact that you had a deep seated reason to wish him ill."

"It took me so long to find him, once he'd changed his name to Aspinal. But as soon as I saw that face in the Ardensis promotional brochure, I recognised him straight away. I never wanted to harm him. I guess as far as it's ever possible to do so, I wanted to forgive him."

"Forgive him? For killing your daughter?" He pauses and leans closer. "You must know, Issy, that no one goes out of their way to change their name without good reason."

I think he's talking about Aspinal. "He had good reason."

"No, Issy. I'm talking about you. You used to go by the name Rachel."

"I never liked it. When I was a child, everyone called me Issy. I just went back to it."

"And you took a job at Ardensis under the name of Isobel Cunningham. To be where Aspinal worked. Why would you do that if the intention was not to deceive?"

"I don't know if I can tell you why I felt the need to be close to him. It's just what I did. Maybe in a strange way it was a means of not forgetting Kelly, of keeping her in my thoughts. I'm no longer sure. "

"Not sure about such a life changing move? Isn't this something else you're choosing not to recall?"

I'm feeling worn down by his questioning. I want it to go away. "I don't understand where this is leading, Inspector."

"Let's go back to Valentine's Day Eve, after you got back from Soho with Mike Aspinal. You're not telling us you still don't remember what happened? After what he did to you. What happened next? How did you get home?"

"Like I told you, there are still blanks. There's a gap until next morning when I'm back in the office and people are looking at me as if something has gone very wrong."

Ives glares at me. "What if I was to tell you that I don't believe you, Issy? What if I was to say that I know you're hiding behind the problems you claim to have with your memory?"

"I don't have to answer questions like that."

"I think you do, Issy. Isn't it true that you planned all along to harm Aspinal for what he did to Kelly?"

I can feel the tears running down my cheeks.

Ives produces a small object in a transparent evidence bag and places it on the table. "Do you recognize this?"

It's the syringe I've seen in my memories of that night. The one that Marianne mentioned.

"It's not something I want to talk about."

"We found it in your desk drawer. Together with a bottle of potassium chloride. Why would you keep such things there if you didn't intend to use them?"

"You tell me."

"You can't recall having them?"

I lie. "No."

"Can't or won't?"

"What do you mean?"

'You see, Issy, Mike Aspinal was killed with a syringe like this. We know it was *this* syringe, the one we found in your desk drawer. It has traces of Mike Aspinal's DNA on the needle tip. Someone's gone to great lengths to wash it out and wipe it clean of fingerprints but they haven't done enough to remove the last traces of Aspinal's blood."

"You're saying I used it to kill him?"

"You realise, don't you Issy, that if someone went to the trouble of cleaning the syringe and removing their prints, then that implies premeditation. It takes away the suggestion that something was done in the heat of the moment. It means something calculating took place. And that makes it murder of the most significant kind. You're quite sure you don't want to tell me anything about that?"

I shake my head. "I never meant him harm."

"After what he did to your daughter? After he'd raped you?"

"You need to believe me, Inspector. It's the hardest lesson I've ever had to learn. If someone's done great harm to you or your loved ones, and you spend the rest of your life hating them, they've won. They've ruined your life. The damage they've done continues. Forgive them and you take that away. Succeed in moving on and you're showing them they can never win."

"But you haven't moved on, have you. Issy? Why else did you take the job at Ardensis? Why choose to place yourself anywhere near a man like Aspinal if you didn't mean to harm him?"

I can feel my resolve weakening. I'm sure I have this straight, that I've had enough time to place these things I can recall in their rightful place. But now, in this moment, facing Ives, I'm becoming less sure. Perhaps Ives is right. Despite what I'm telling him, I know I hated Aspinal enough to kill him. I've seen the syringe in my hands. It's just a short step to admitting that I used it to kill him.

I make the only reply I know how to make. "I don't think it was anything like you're saying it was."

Ives continues without hearing me. "And that's why you searched for information on the Internet about death by lethal injection."

"If you say so."

"Why you visited your friend Mary Duggan and stole potassium chloride from her lab."

He's on the point convincing me he's right. I've blocked out so many of these thoughts from my mind. Yes, I wanted Aspinal dead. Yes, I got hold of the syringe. Yes, I searched the Internet for how to use it. Yes, I stole the chemicals from Mary's lab. It's all true.

"Yes, Inspector."

"You admit to killing Mike Aspinal?"

I fall silent. I'm confused by everything Ives is putting to me. If what he says is true, then I killed Mike. And my memories of that night that have come back to me are telling me that is so. Yet I don't feel like the killer Ives is making me out to be.

How would a killer feel? I know I wanted to kill Mike Aspinal. Everything about that is true. Yes, I feel like someone who wanted to kill. Wanted that with every fibre of my body. But do I know what it's like to kill? I can't be sure. It doesn't feel like I do.

Ives bangs the table and startles me. "Did you hear the question, Issy? Did you kill Mike Aspinal?"

I still say nothing. I'm transfixed, caught in a trap, unable to move.

The door of the interview room opens.

Ives looks to the skies.

DS Lesley enters and whispers something in his ear.

He turns to me. "I'm going to give you time to think, Issy. Think carefully. Matters will go a whole lot better for you if you admit to what you've done."

As he begins to walk away, I call him back. "Tell me, did Marianne French lead you to the coffee bar?"

"That really matters to you at a time like this?"

"It does, Inspector."

He gives a smile. "No, she didn't. We had you in our sights from the moment you stepped off the train at Old Street."

He leaves me alone in the room.

I can hear the door being locked from the outside.

# CHAPTER 77

I know I was on the point of saying 'yes' to Ives but the realisation that this would make me a killer caused me to stop.

He pushed me further than I ever wanted to go in reliving the events surrounding Mike Aspinal's death. And now, as I sit here alone in the interview room, I find my thoughts turning once more to the events of Valentine's Eve.

I'm back again at Ardensis. The night Mike raped me.

*I'm hurting and in pain. He's gorged himself on the violence he's shown me. Become the beast that had been in hiding within him. Wrecked my life for a second time.*

*He deserves to die.*

*I'm crying. Collapsed on the chair at the desk in my workspace.*

*Somewhere, back in his office, Aspinal must be congratulating himself on his night's work.*

*Yes, he deserves to die. Yet I feel so weak. Do I have the strength?*

*I reach into the desk drawer and search for the drawstring tie bag in the false compartment I've made in the bottom drawer.*

*I open the bag and place the syringe on the desk. I open the bottle that holds the potassium chloride and draw the liquid into the syringe. No need to worry about air pockets. If he gets embolism along with the dose of potassium chloride, so much the better.*

*I stare at the filled syringe. Come on, Issy. You can do this. He deserves it. If you don't do this now, he'll do it again. To someone else. Others will suffer. Your chance to finish him now.*

*He deserves it for what he did to Kelly. My sweet, innocent Kelly.*

*You only have to go back to the office. Make some excuse. He'll be disarmed by his success. Get close enough to him. Spike him with the needle. Push in the liquid. Watch him contort and convulse. Spit on him as he dies.*

*I drop the syringe back to the desktop.*

*I know I can't do it. I'll go to the police. I'll tell them what he's done. They'll see that I get justice.*

*There's a sound in the corridor outside.*

*It must be Mike, coming for me again.*

*I take hold of the loaded syringe. If he comes in, I'll use it to defend myself.*

*The door opens.*

*It's Vince Blakemore.*

*"Issy. What's happening?"*

*"You're not meant to be here."*

*"Well, here I am. What's Mike done to you?"*

*"Can't you see?"*

*He looks long and hard at the syringe that I'm holding in my hand. "And that was going to be your answer?"*

*"I can't. I want to. He deserves it. But I can't do it."*

*Vince takes the syringe and holds it in his left hand. "Go home, Issy. Leave this to me."*

The memory fades. I know this is something I won't need to see again.

I know now that I'm no killer. No matter what Ives might be saying.

But I know that Aspinal deserved to die.

I just wasn't strong enough to do it myself.

Blakemore removed Aspinal from my life, the man who caused me so much pain. Not only by killing my precious child, but also by defiling me and caring nothing about the suffering he caused.

I owe a debt of gratitude to Vince Blakemore. He snuffed out a worthless soul that deserves no place in this world.

What if I tell Ives the truth? Ives might believe me. I would be relieved to clear my name. But, in this moment, the feeling that this is the right thing to do will not come. Something in me hopes that Ives would not believe me. That way, Vince Blakemore would remain safe.

Ives and his team are thorough. If I say anything, they're bound to uncover the truth. Then I'll be giving evidence against Vince, the man who made the world come straight for me.

I think back to my time with my mother in our home in Reading, in the wake of her despair at the way I let my father know that she'd been unfaithful. I broke the trust she placed in me then and that could never be repaired.

How can I denounce Vince and condemn him to a lifetime in prison for what he did in straightening out the world for me? He never asked for my trust. But the look that passed between us when he took the syringe from me and went into Aspinal's office to kill the man was a silent agreement as strong any we could ever have made.

It's time to honour that trust.

And, for the first time in my life, to trust myself.

I look over at the large mirror on the wall. If not Ives, there would be someone watching me from there.

I give a wave that says: *I'm ready to talk.*

# CHAPTER 78

Ives is incandescent. Lesley had interrupted the questioning of Issy Cunningham at a critical moment. "She was about to confess, June. And then you walked in."

"I'm sorry, Steve. It couldn't wait. Marianne French had something important to tell us."

She tells him about her interview with Marianne. "French was genuine, I'm sure of that. She told me she'd seen the syringe and a bottle of potassium chloride in Cunningham's desk drawer. Days before the murder."

Ives bristles with anger. "Genuine, you say. And yet she told no one?"

"She did tell someone, Steve. She told Colin Tempest."

"And not the police?"

Lesley shakes her head. "No. She didn't have any answer to that."

"So, what's the big concern, anyway? Marianne French is a witness to say that Cunningham had the syringe and the potassium chloride in her possession. It strengthens the case."

Lesley looks down. "There's something you need to know, Steve. Something you're not going to like. Something I discovered yesterday but put on one side. Something that came into focus once I heard what Marianne French had to say." She pauses to take a deep breath. "There's another entrance to the Ardensis offices. It's on the second floor. It's never used. The idea was that cleaners could come and go that way without being on show in the main foyer. They stopped using it a couple of years back when a new cleaning company, Acre Cleaning, took over the contract. They insisted on using the front entrance. Something about health and safety and getting their equipment in and out. The second floor entrance was locked and no one knows anything about the key. And here's the important thing, Steve, there are no security cameras trained on that entrance."

"So, you're suggesting that anyone who had the key could have been in there at the time of the murder?"

"It has to be a possibility."

"Tell me two things, June. How come I didn't know about this? And what did you do to find out about it?"

"Just being thorough, Steve. I called Acre Cleaning. Asked them how they got their people in and out of the building. They were very helpful. Told me about the health and safety issue and how they'd been told to not use the second floor entrance. I then checked our security cameras that faced the building and found that the entrance isn't covered. But I didn't know then how important this might be."

Ives tousles his hair. "So, you're saying there could be a big hole in my case against Cunningham."

Lesley chimes in. "It's *our* case, Steve."

"Let's park that for awhile, June. You're saying that Cunningham and Aspinal might not have been alone on the night of the murder. But you have no proof of that. And you can't deny that Cunningham was all along planning to kill Aspinal. She had the syringe ready. Now Marianne French is ready to support that, the case is stronger."

"We don't know that someone else didn't use it and then leave it in Cunningham's desk drawer to incriminate her. Someone cleared up after themselves. It's hard to believe that Cunningham was capable of that after what she'd just been through."

Ives tries to laugh. "You don't give up, do you, June? Nothing's going to shake your faith in this woman."

"We can't prove she used the syringe, Steve. We can only prove she had it in her possession."

"Like I said, you never give up."

"Just trying to put myself in the shoes of Cunningham's defence team. We need to have answers to questions like this if we're going to make the charge against her stick. That's all I'm thinking."

Ives stands and prepares to leave the room. "June. Let's just concentrate on convicting Cunningham. Once she confesses, I'm sure these issues you're raising won't have anything like as much importance."

# CHAPTER 79

By the time Ives returns to face me over the interview room table, my mind is made up. I need to make no mistakes in convincing him that I killed Mike Aspinal.

He's being careful. The interview is being recorded and filmed. He wants it to be clear to all that he isn't pressuring me into a confession. At the same time, I know I have to give no hint that I now know I'm innocent. Without a word being spoken, we collude in presenting a case that no jury would disbelieve.

He opens with a smile. "I'm sorry, Issy, for the interruption. At least you've had time to think about all that I put to you."

I nod in agreement.

He continues. "Murder is the most serious crime. I want you to think carefully before answering. Did you kill Mike Aspinal?"

I take my time. "He deserved it, Inspector. No one should be allowed to act as he did."

"You mean the killing of your daughter? You know the court decided that was an accident?"

"Then why didn't he stop?"

"That was taken into account when he was sentenced."

"Six months. Do you think that was anything like enough?"

He doesn't answer. "Or maybe you're saying he deserved to die because of what he did to you?"

"Well, didn't he?"

"It doesn't matter what I think, Issy."

"Then, yes. He deserved to die for thinking that he could do with people as he wishes and there would be no comebacks. The world can't be like that, Inspector."

"So, you righted the wrongs."

"As far as they could ever be righted."

"And that meant killing Mike Aspinal?"

"Yes, I killed him. I was hurt and crying in such distress after he raped me. I felt I had no strength to go on. But then I thought, why should a man like that be able to get away with what he's done? So, I took the syringe from my desk drawer, filled it and went back into his office. He looked at me with such disdain as I stood before him. I don't know what pathetic thoughts were passing through his warped mind in that moment but he wasn't scared of me. Quite the opposite. I think he might even have been expecting me to be grateful to him in some way that he'd abused me. So, I came closer and jabbed him with the syringe, pushed the fluid in quickly before he even knew what was happening. I saw him collapse and fall to the floor. I stood over him and watched as he contorted and died a slow death."

"Where did you stab him? Where did the needle land?"

"I don't recall."

"But that's something you must know."

"In his chest. I thrust out and that's where it caught him. I'm more or less sure of that. But you have to realise, Inspector, that I was in no fit state to be worried about that. I only cared that I had him. That I gave him what he deserved."

"What did you do then?"

"After I'd watched him die? I took the syringe back to my desk, cleaned it, placed it back where I kept it hidden."

"Why would you do that, if you'd acted in distress?"

"I don't know. Maybe it's because I wasn't able to think straight. It's what I did. That's all there is to it."

Ives leans forward. "And you acted alone?"

"Yes, Inspector. There was no one else there that night. It was me. I killed him."

"You admit to killing Mike Aspinal?"

"Yes."

"Then I have to repeat the caution. You have the right to remain silent. Anything you say may be used as evidence against you. Failure to reply may be taken into account. Do you understand?"

I nod. "Yes. I'm glad he's gone, Inspector. Glad he got what was coming to him."

Ives produces a typed document he has ready prepared.

He slips the words out almost as a whisper. "I charge you with the murder of Michael Aspinal." He pauses to show me the document. "I want you to read this carefully, Issy. It says you confess to the murder of Aspinal. It lists the items of evidence that we've discussed. If you sign you'll be agreeing that this is a true statement."

I don't look at what he's showing me for long. I pick up the pen that Ives offers and sign my name.

# CHAPTER 80

Ives finds Lesley in the incident room. She's removing the photos from the white board she's been maintaining since the start of the investigation.

"You're not exactly elated, June. Why not lighten up? We have Cunningham's confession. Time to go for a beer and celebrate. Drink to the good health of the Commissioner and another serious crime put to bed."

Lesley turns round to face him. "Just picking away at the loose ends, Steve."

"What loose ends? Don't tell me you're still defending Cunningham? Not now."

"Tempest and Blakemore both have a motive, Steve. Colin Tempest needed money to pay off his gambling debts. Aspinal was making that impossible. He had everything to gain from Aspinal's death."

"And Blakemore?"

"Why did he come back into the country without anyone knowing? Why did he lie about that? We know he was in London on the morning of the murder. Aspinal was helping Justin Hardman take over Ardensis, the company that Blakemore had worked half his life to make a success. We know that now the emails have been de-encrypted. With Aspinal out of the way, the takeover couldn't go ahead. Very convenient for Blakemore."

Ives tries to laugh. "You don't give up, do you, June? Nothing's going to shake your faith in this woman's innocence. But why stop there? Why stop at Tempest and Blakemore? Why not add Justin Hardman to the list? Maybe Aspinal was about to double cross him.

Maybe that meant that Hardman needed to kill him, even though the deal would no longer go through. Too many maybes, June. Too many maybes."

"Hardman's no longer with us, Steve."

"No one's going to be at all concerned about the loss of Hardman and Taylor. Must have had enough enemies to get killed a hundred times over." He pauses. "Anyhow, it doesn't mean Hardman can't be one of your suspects, if you're casting the net as wide as you are. June, the fact of the matter is that you have no real evidence for any of this. You're still dealing with possibilities when I'm dealing with facts. Cunningham has confessed and the details of that confession match the evidence."

"Down to where the needle entered Aspinal's body?"

"Her recall of events is bound to be confused. We know that. In the heat of the moment, it's almost inevitable that she would be wrong on some of the fine detail."

"Which means the evidence is not one hundred per cent."

"Nothing in this world is one hundred per cent, June. You know that."

"She's taking a fall, Steve. I'm certain of it. I don't know for who but every instinct I have tells me that's what's happening. You know how a jury is going to have this presented to it. Injured woman. Spur of the moment. Extreme provocation. Enough sympathetic drag to make a short sentence inevitable. I don't like it, Steve. It's all working out too well for someone, somewhere. You have to be suspicious."

"Don't overcomplicate this, June. You have to put it away. We have our killer. She's led us a merry dance and we finally have her, confession and all. You're going to have to admit that I was right about her all along."

Lesley says no more as she tears up the photos and drops them in the bin.

# EPILOGUE

Adam and Mary were waiting when I was released from Holloway Prison.

I wrapped my arms around them and thanked them for all they did for me, the risks they took on my behalf.

Once I confessed to the killing, no action was taken against either of them, other than a stern warning from Ives about wasting police time.

In prison, I had more than enough time to think about what I did and I became ever more certain that it was right and that I would do the same again.

Mike Aspinal had to be stopped. There was justice in that. No more lives would be ruined.

The calculation I made in confessing to the killing was that any sentence I received would be trivial compared with anything that might be handed down to Vince Blakemore. I was provoked into killing the man. Vince would have been accused of acting in cold-blooded recrimination for a challenge to his business.

In English law, murder can never be overlooked, whatever the provocation. Ives had produced clear evidence of premeditation, giving Judge Haliday no choice but to confer a minimum sentence, or tariff, on me of eighteen years. My heart sank when I stood in the dock and heard this.

But Judge Haliday went on to say that there were mitigating circumstances in this case. She recognised that by pleading guilty, I recognised the magnitude of my crime and expressed regret. She also told the court that there was a strong element of provocation as a result of the rape and that without Aspinal's criminal behaviour in this respect, the murder, though planned, may never have taken place. She understood my feelings of anger at the death of my daughter, Kelly, but warned that revenge has no place in a law abiding society.

I held my breath as she prepared to tell the court what was the effect of these mitigating circumstances. When she announced the final sentence as five years and six months, I felt a wave of relief. With good behaviour, a parole board could reduce this by up to fifty per cent.

And there I was, walking back to freedom after just three years. Three long years but so much shorter than the initial eighteen year tariff.

Before my release, the shortest time served for murder in England was three years and eight months.

I became a record holder of a kind I never would have anticipated or wished for.

I returned to work at Ardensis and was greeted by Vince Blakemore with a knowing look on my first day back.

During the three years I was away, he initiated a programme employing ex-offenders and now had three working for the company. There was nothing suspicious in my becoming ex-offender number four.

He welcomed me into his office. The place where Aspinal had died now looked different. Vince had changed the layout, installed new furniture and brightened the place. Yet nothing could disguise for me the terrible events that took place there.

When we were alone with the door closed, he confided in me. "I know what you did for me, Issy. How can I ever repay you?"

I held up my hand. "No, Vince. It's you I have to thank."

There was now an unbreakable understanding between us.

One day, when talking about what bound us together, Vince said enough to let me know that he was behind the killing of Hardman and Taylor.

I realised then that he not only avenged Kelly's death but that he also rid the world of two more souls who deserved no place in it.

And in so doing, Vince Blakemore saved my life.

Yet, there is one thing still troubling me. Why did he replace the syringe in my desk drawer after he used it? Had he all along made the calculation that this would lead me to confess and allow him to get away with murder?"

Trust. That short, short word.

Also by Seb Kirby:

# EACH DAY I WAKE
## A gripping psychological thriller

Young women are going missing and only Tom Markland knows the terrifying truth. When he's pulled out of the North Dock, he comes round not knowing who he is or how he got there. All he knows is that someone is killing young women. He sees them die each time he closes his eyes. The only way he's going to recover his identity is to discover who is doing the killings. **Each Day I Wake** will keep you turning page after page.

**What reviewers are saying about EACH DAY I WAKE:**

"A thrilling page turner of a book."

"The crisp dialogue and unexpected twists and turns in the plot kept me interested all the way to the devastating ending."

"A brilliantly written twisting thriller that I couldn't put down."

"Engulfing, suspenseful...will keep you guessing."

"This really is a cracking good read."

"A cleverly-crafted plot that draws you in from page one."

"I loved this one... A captivating and compelling read!"

"An enjoyable fast paced thriller. Lots of twists and turns."

"A great roller coaster of a read...."

Further details here: http://smarturl.it/ediw

## Acknowledgements

I would like to express my thanks to Tracy Fenton and everyone at the THE Book Club for all their interest and support.

Cover design is by Jane Dixon-Smith (http://www.jdsmith-design.com).

Made in the USA
Charleston, SC
29 September 2016